Christmas Tales
THAT WARM THE HEART

VOLUME I

SHARON CHARLES

Abundant Living Ministries

Christmas Tales that warm the heart
Volume I

© 2019 by Sharon Charles

ISBN-13: 978-0-9759019-9-1
ISBN-10: 0-9759019-9-0

Abundant Living Ministries
541 W 28th Division Hwy
Lititz, PA 17543
AbundantLivingMinistries.org
email: info@AbundantLivingMinistries.org

Table of Contents

Introduction 1

The Staircase 3

All About Figuring Out 19

Christmas Annie 29

The Other Side of the Fence 41

Timing is Everything 55

More than a Sparrow 69

Charlie's Song 85

After the Curtain Fell 97

The Christmas Sack 107

All Santa Wanted 135

Yumi, the Flea 159

Something Much Better 177

Dedication

To my husband John
who is my very best friend, editor, and fan.
How blessed I am
to have your love and encouragement.

And to amazing children and grandchildren
who warm my heart not just at Christmas
but every day of the year!

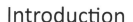

Introduction

Reading to my children was always a favorite family tradition... especially during the Christmas season. So, one December, I decided to write my own story to read to the youngsters.

They really liked that first tale, which inspired me to write another the following year. Soon the stories became an annual tradition. Some were based on true events from my childhood. A few started with snippets of fact which then took on a life of their own. And, a few others were pure fantasy.

Fact and fiction, they all contained a little real life here, a little make-believe there. But each one aimed at making the first Christmas, and its significance, just a bit more understandable and relevant to our children.

The stories began to circulate beyond our family. Friends asked when the next would be finished. Strangers wrote to say they had laughed and cried. Annie and Charlie, whiskered Walt, Yumi the flea, and others had captured their hearts. Or perhaps it was Jesus who captured their hearts!

Twenty-five years have flown by and friends have been urging the publication of these tales. This first volume contains twelve of the stories and, Lord willing,

will be followed next year with a second volume of others.

It's now our grandchildren begging Grandma to read. They need the same Savior their parents did. May these stories be one more way of pointing them toward HIM.

So, by a warm fire, or wherever we can manage to curl up together, I will be reading these tales again, and again, and again.

And now I hope you will too!

The Staircase

The top of the stairs...no doubt about it! That was *my* place! When I was only four years old, my parents started calling it "Lizzie's Lair at the top of the stair." I didn't even know what that meant, but I liked the sound of it!

Every child has a favorite place in the home in which they grow up. For some it's the cluttered pantry full of tins and jars, fruits and spices, mops and buckets. For others it's the attic inhabited by trunks and boxes, old furniture and broken lamps, bats and mothballs. Still others love to retreat to the fuzzy dust balls under their very own bed, or to the weed-infested corner of the backyard, or maybe even the coat closet among the boots and smelly sneakers. But for me... Elizabeth Catherine Clarke, better known to my family and friends as "Lizzie"... my special place was definitely at the top of the steps!

It was a marvelous staircase. No ordinary flight of steps. Today people would say it had character. The lower three-fourths of the stairway separated two large rooms, the kitchen on one side and the living room on the other. There was a comfortably-worn railing on

3

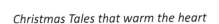

both sides with curvy wooden spindles. The railing had been sat upon, slid down, slapped, and squeezed and even bore my teeth marks here and there! The spindles were at times my jail bars; at other times, they became window frames through which I tried to press my eyes, nose and mouth, in order to glimpse what was going on in the room below.

The treads of the steps were worn nicely in the middle. In places, the old carpet runner was threadbare and the yellowed wooden floor showed through. I had bottom-bumped down those steps on many occasions. And, in pre-Home Alone fashion, I had once tobogganed down them on an old scrap of tin... much to my mother's disapproval! I had climbed them with every emotion of life. In times of light-heartedness my feet barely touched them as I flew up or down. In hard times, my feet felt cemented to each tread, and it took all the strength I could muster to drag my body upstairs. At night, even when I was all properly hugged and kissed, prayed with, and tucked into bed in my second-floor room, I imagined all kinds of horrors coming up those steps. The creaks could be monsters from outer space, communists invading from Cuba or burglars about to murder me in my sleep. It was creepy but tingly and exciting too! How I loved those steps!

What I liked most was the top four steps. These were walled on both sides and therefore were completely hidden from the rooms below and the rooms above. I could sit on those steps and eavesdrop on unsuspecting family members. They never knew I was there! I would curl up there and daydream to my heart's content, absolutely alone in my own private world. And it was at the top of those steps that I learned four of life's most terrible and wonderful truths.

The first lesson was learned at age five. I suppose I was a lot like most five-year-olds growing up in the 50's, although perhaps with an over-active imagination! I liked worms and baseball, climbing trees and fighting with my older brothers. God had created the world to revolve around me... at least that's what I figured. I didn't have one serious care and, if by some strange chance anything nasty were ever to happen, I was certain Dad and Mom would fix it. Isn't that what parents were for?

We got the call from England late one night. It was so unusual to hear the shrill ring of the telephone at such an unearthly hour that I hopped out of bed and crept over to my favorite spot at the top of the steps, so I could hear what was being said in the kitchen below. I could tell, as my father asked somber questions in a shaky voice, that something he was hearing wasn't good. When he hung up the receiver I overheard him tell my mother that my favorite Uncle Jim had suffered a heart attack while vacationing in Europe and wasn't expected to live!

This was absolutely inconceivable to me... that my wonderful, healthy, kind Uncle Jim could die. Favorite people shouldn't die! He wouldn't! I pressed my face into my knees and prayed that he would live. God would make him live. I was sure.

But two nights later came the phone call that shattered my safe little world. Huddled once again at the top of the steps, I heard the bitter announcement... Uncle Jim was dead!

I guess my parents thought that a five-year-old should be sheltered from death, because they said very little about it to me, and did not take me to the "funeral parlor" or the "funeral." These were very puzzling words. I had no pictures to put with them in my mind. They were just bad things associated with a never-to-be-seen-again dear Uncle Jim. And at the top of the steps while everyone else went to this funeral-thing, I sat at home crying on the top step while the baby-sitter read a novel in the living room below. Death, although little understood, became a reality to me. And life seemed not quite so nice as before, even at the top of the steps.

The second lesson was not painful as the first. It happened when I was eight. There was a knock at our kitchen door early one evening. I ran to open it. There stood Dr. Williams, our silver-bearded family doctor. I was always a little scared of him... probably because of the shots and disgusting-tasting medicine he had inflicted on me in the past. But I was feeling fine and healthy this particular evening and so was everyone else in the family. So why was he at our door? My father hurriedly appeared and whisked the doctor up the stairs. I followed right on their heels but, at the top of the steps, my father stopped abruptly, turned and informed me in his "don't-you-dare-disobey-me" voice that I should wait downstairs. I started back down the steps but, as soon as Dad had disappeared, I reclaimed my favorite spot where I strained to hear what was going on in the upstairs master bedroom. I heard nothing.

I concluded Mom must be the sick person. I knew she had been resting most of the day. Now I wondered if she would die like Uncle Jim had. The steps seemed very cold and lonely right then. For hours I stretched across the top step, with one leg hanging down, napping periodically and waking impatiently, wondering why Dr. Williams was staying so long.

"Mom must be terribly ill, or he would have come down ages ago," I thought. "How long could it take the doc to take her temperature, give her a shot, and prescribe some pills, dry toast and tea or ginger ale, just like he always did?"

Suddenly, his patent-leather shoe descended almost right on my head! He was as surprised to see me on the top step, as I was startled out of my dreadful doze. He grabbed my hand, helped me to my feet and then said the most surprising thing. "Lizzie, I've just left you a little brother upstairs with your mother," he announced with a wink and gentle pat on the head. "I think his name's Jimmy." And with that, he squeezed by me on the stairway and disappeared out the kitchen door.

Now this was back in the days when "pregnant" was next to a swear word! And having babies, though a natural occurrence, was an unnaturally-taboo subject of conversation. I had been totally unaware that there was a baby on the way. Pretty dumb, huh? I just couldn't figure out how the doctor had managed to smuggle a baby past me! And for some reason, my parents wouldn't answer any of my questions on that topic. But if nothing else, there on the top step I learned the lesson that life keeps on going and that, for the Uncle Jims who die, there are precious new lives born to take their place. Life on the top step seemed to sparkle with a little more fun and mischief once again!

The third lesson happened when I was ten. I was always getting into scrapes of one kind or another, usually because of my stubborn disobedience. My mother had often told me she hoped someday I would have a kid just as ornery as I had been... so I could experience some of what I had put her through! I was the kind of child who would ask a total stranger why she had wrinkles in her skin, or tell a relative that my parents couldn't stand him. I'm sure I was a parent's nightmare!

This particular day I was caught in an outright lie to my mother. She had preached at me ever since birth that God sees me all the time and that, although I could lie to her, God would always know the truth. But since God is invisible, I was quite successful at ignoring His existence. I did my mischief, told my little inaccuracies and tried to ignore the irritating conscience that agreed with my mother.

You would like to know the lie, wouldn't you? What morbid curiosity! Well, it didn't seem like such a big deal to me. I simply told my mother that I had come straight home from school that day. The truth was that, since I knew she was not going to be at home for a few hours, I suggested to my friend that we go play in the park for

a while. We had a great time and I made sure that I still arrived home before my mother. I had a vague awareness that she probably wouldn't have approved of two ten-year-olds playing alone at the community park. But since nothing terrible had happened, I was confident Mom would never know the difference. I hadn't counted on my friend's mother discovering the truth and immediately calling to inform my mother. From the top of the steps I eavesdropped on yet another phone conversation. Mom's tone was stern... I knew I was in for it!

Sure enough. I was banished to my room for the rest of the evening, to contemplate the seriousness of my crime. Being a social creature at heart, it was a fitting punishment to make me spend time in solitude. However, that verdict sentenced me to something much worse than loneliness. It turned out to be a bitterly sad night because that was the evening my father arrived home with a new puppy for the family! I heard my siblings squealing with delight in the kitchen below. And I definitely heard the adorable little yelps from the pup! I sneaked out of my bedroom, creeping carefully to my spot at the top of the steps. Lying on my stomach I could peek through the top spindles without my parents catching me. Watching my family play with that dog, and even choose its name without my participation, was torture! I vowed I would never lie again. The reality of judgment for sin struck home with painful intensity, there at the top of the steps!

You would think that after that lesson, I would have turned over a new leaf and become the perfect kid but, much to my parents' concern, I didn't. Actually, there were no really big offenses for quite some time. Then at Christmastime when I turned eleven, the greatest lesson of all was learned.

As usual, I was to take part in the annual Christmas Eve program at church. I was to play the part of an angel... how totally unsuited to my personality!

The evening of the program I got to the church basement ahead of many of the cast. My dad was an incurable early arriver! So I tossed my coat on one of the Sunday School tables and wandered around the Junior department, awaiting the arrival of more kids. Over in the corner were two tables. One was piled high with cans of soup, boxes of macaroni, and scads of other food items. I remembered that one of the youth classes was gathering items for the city mission. On the table right beside this collection, there was one item which caught my attention. It was a colorful, crystal-studded, rectangular-shaped tin... fascinatingly beautiful. I had seen one just like it the week before when shopping with my mother. I knew it contained those yummy new

Cadbury cookies shaped like fingers and dipped in milk chocolate. How I wished to have that beautiful tin along with its delicious contents! Five minutes earlier I never would have dreamed that I would do what I did... but before I could really think about my stupidity, I grabbed my coat from the other table and threw it over that tin. I figured it was just one more item for the mission, simply placed on the wrong table. Those poor homeless souls wouldn't know that they were getting shorted one box of cookies. I could sneak the tin home under my coat after the program and savor those cookies later that night.

Within minutes the basement came alive with play participants, throwing their coats on top of mine and scurrying around to don halos and wings, bathrobes and sandals. In the busy-ness, I temporarily forgot about the tin.

The Sunday School superintendent seemed in a real tizzy, but she always seemed a little unraveled in the head to me, so I didn't think much about it.

Finally, we were performing our parts on the crowded platform. We were all doing quite well too, in my opinion. The church was exceptionally pretty! It was poinsettia-ed to the hilt, and candled way beyond to-day's fire codes. Christmas really had almost a fantasy-world effect on me and probably on all the others too. The stillness and reverence seemed to inspire us. We pulled off our acting better than at any of the practices.

The Staircase

We angels sang angelically to the shepherds. The shepherds did their hasty travel to Bethlehem and knelt in awe before the manger. Then the narrator announced the arrival of the wise men from the east. Three primary department boys with foil-covered cardboard crowns and magic-markered beards paraded solemnly up the center aisle. One by one they moved in front of the primitive spotlight fixed on the manger. As the first one stepped into the light he held high his gift of gold... it was actually a shoe box wrapped in gold florist foil, but it looked expensive. The second magi stepped into the light and held up his gift of frankincense... it was actually some old bottle that had been painted in a sort of stained glass effect, but pretty impressive-looking to my 11-year-old eyes. Finally, the third sage stepped rather tentatively into the light. Looking down from my angel post, I could see immediately that he looked very uncomfortable. Although he held his hands out in the gesture of giving, there was nothing in his hands. They were completely empty. Where was the myrrh? Probably the Sunday School superintendent had lost it... no wonder she was in a stew! Or maybe the kid had left it at home... his mother was probably pretty mad at him!

And then it dawned on me... not in my brain, but in the pit of my stomach. I gulped guiltily as the shocking realization rolled over me. I was the culprit... *I had stolen the myrrh!* Oh no! It was bad enough that I had

stolen cookies from the poor, now I had stolen from baby Jesus Himself!

I squirmed and fidgeted and wished I could run and hide. I imagined that everyone in the room knew what I had done. Of course, they didn't know... but I was certain my face revealed my guilt. I couldn't wait for the program to be over! As quickly as possible (after the final "sleep in heavenly peace" was sung), I ran to the base- ment and changed from my costume. I dug my coat and cookie tin out from under the mountain of other coats. Miserably, I hid the tin under my jacket, pinching it under my arm. It never even occurred to me to just leave it there, or place it with the mission items. It seemed too late for that... I figured I was stuck with the myrrh for the rest of my life. And bitter myrrh it was!

I was silent on the ride home. This undoubtedly raised considerable suspicion in my parents' minds. Whenever I quit talking, I was usually up to no good, or sick. By the time we arrived home, they were convinced something was wrong. My mother felt my head to see if I was coming down with something. No such luck! Then the inevitable happened... they noticed the bulge under my coat. At that point, I was just too tired and frustrated to think up a good lie. Besides, I'd learned that lesson before, remember? I could have told them it was a Christmas gift from Mrs. Jenkins, the flustered Sunday School supcrintendent. Or I could have told

them I'd bought it as a gift for them and now that they had found it, the secret was ruined. Wouldn't that have been something? I could have put them on a guilt trip for even thinking of accusing me of wrong-doing!

I could have pulled any of a number of cons that kids are great at but for some reason I just wanted to confess the whole rotten mess. I wanted to be rid of the myrrh! I'd ripped off baby Jesus! How much lower could I get? I was so very, very sorry!

Tearfully I confessed my Cadbury crime to my parents there in the kitchen. They listened, stone-faced and then told me to go to my room to wait until they could decide my punishment. As I trudged up the staircase, my special staircase, it seemed steeper than usual. Those last four steps felt cold and unfriendly. I changed into PJ's, crawled under my covers and listened for the dreadful creaks that would mean my sentence was approaching.

Sure enough, it wasn't long until I heard my father's footsteps. How menacing they sounded! He knocked three times on my bedroom door and then entered. I braced myself for the announcement. I knew that even at eleven years of age, I probably wasn't beyond getting a good paddling... wouldn't that be an awful way to spend Christmas Eve?

To my amazement, Dad smiled tenderly and sat down on the edge of my bed. Then he slowly pulled from his pocket one gigantic orange. To a young girl like me in the late 50's, an orange was considered a rare and expensive treat. My eyes bulged. What on earth was that orange for?

In a gentle voice he asked, "Lizzie, would you like this orange?"

Would I? If I hadn't been feeling like such low-down scum, I would have grabbed it from him right away. "Yes," I answered meekly. "But I don't deserve any gift right now."

"No, you don't. You did wrong tonight. But your mother and I love you in spite of what you did. We forgive you and want to bless you by giving you this orange."

I hadn't anticipated this kind of reaction. I couldn't figure it out.

My Dad continued, "It was Jesus that you stole from tonight, but you've been stealing from Him for a long time, you know."

"I have?" What was Dad driving at?

"I hope you will soon realize that, when you try to keep running your life yourself, you're really robbing

the God who created you. He wants to forgive you for all the wrong things you've done and even more than that, He wants to give you contentment. That is a far more valuable gift than this orange. He loves you... even more than your mother and I do. He died for you, you know." He placed the orange in my hands and pressed my fingers around it. Then he bent over and kissed me. And that was it. He left. The steps creaked much more gently than they had sounded moments earlier and I was left to ponder his lesson of forgiveness.

I fell asleep, clutching the orange and mulling over the events of the evening, wondering if I could ever really get to know God like my parents seemed to know Him.

When the first rays of sunlight hit my bed, I jumped up. It was Christmas! I grabbed the orange from my bed and tiptoed from my room. I always liked to get downstairs before the rest of the family on Christmas morning. Just as I started down the top four steps of my precious staircase I stopped short and stared. There on the wall was something amazing. The early morning sun, slanting through the kitchen window below, had produced a clear shadow on the wall. In later years I realized it had probably come from an unused roll of Christmas wrap propped against the staircase railing. But on that Christmas morning, all I knew was that I was staring at a striking shadow of a cross. I sank down on my step and just kept gazing at that perfect

cross. Then I looked down at the orange still clutched in my hands. Somehow, for the first time, I understood God's forgiveness like I never had before. My parents had forgiven me for stealing the myrrh and had demonstrated their forgiveness with the gift of the orange. God also offered me forgiveness and demonstrated it with the sacrificial gift of His Son. There it was... the cross... proof of God's love... sharply displayed on the wall of my special place! I sat there deep in thought until the rising sun caused the shadow to fade. I began to talk to the Lord because I actually wanted to. He seemed so real and so close. I confessed my dreadful self-centeredness and thanked Him for His gift of salvation. I gave my heart to Him that Christmas morning, right there on the steps.

Sounds in the bedrooms above alerted me that the rest of the family was rousing from sleep. I savored the last few moments of solitude on the staircase. This really was quite the place. Here I had laughed and listened, dreamed and dreaded. Here I had learned lessons of life... and death... and judgment. Now I had discovered the reality of God's mercy and forgiveness too. I smiled and took a big whiff of the orange in my hands. How fitting that I should finally arrive at the foot of the cross... *right here at the top of the steps!*

All About
Figuring Out

Clarence was one terrific cat! So was Papa Bear! They were the only cats I ever really liked... but then... they were different from other cats.

Most cats I never could figure out. When I was six years old, a savage tom clawed my arm simply because I was trying to rescue him from homelessness! Just because a freckle-faced, scrawny, toothless boy crawls under a bush, grabs a feline front paw and starts to drag the animal through some twigs and thistles... did it have to start hissing and scratching? I didn't think so.

Then when I was seven, a Siamese attacked me. I was simply investigating its swaying tail... well, maybe I did hold on a little tightly, but was that any reason to get nasty? I never could figure cats out.

Only Papa Bear and Clarence made sense to me. It seemed that Papa Bear had always lived at our house. As long as I could remember (in my long 10 years of life), he had been there. He was huge and black, with a white patch right where I guessed his heart was. If a cat could look kingly, Papa Bear did. He didn't walk... he strutted! He always appeared to know exactly where he was going on those massive paws and why. The back of our living

room sofa was his throne. Since it was positioned smack in front of a large picture window, he would perch there all day and not miss a thing. It gave him perfect view of happenings inside the house as well as outside on the street. When anyone sat on the sofa, Papa Bear would curl his wonderful tail around their neck. Some folks got quite nervous about this; I think they were afraid he might tighten that tail like a boa constrictor and strangle them. If they would have only realized that Papa Bear wouldn't hurt anyone... he was simply trying to be affectionate (which is quite unusual for a cat, I thought)!

Clarence was Papa Bear's son. At least that's what we imagined. Clarence had just showed up on our door-step one day when I was nine and immediately became my best pal. He looked exactly like a younger, thinner version of Papa Bear, including the white patch over his heart. And he and Papa Bear were instant friends... like they must have known each other already. Clarence was a little more lively than his papa. He'd sit on the sofa back for a while each day, but then he was off exploring, sometimes in the house and often out on the street. I worried about him wandering off so much and couldn't understand why he wasn't satisfied to just enjoy the good life inside. But Clarence seemed like he just had to go. At least he always came back... except last year, right before Christmas!

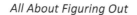

I remember exactly! It was December 21... just four days before Christmas. I was ten years old and really looking forward to the holidays. Our family was busy like every other with shopping, decorating, cooking. And of course, eating! I loved the eating part of Christmas! Why couldn't we have cookies like that all year long? I ate lots of cookies in December and felt perfectly fine, so why did Mom always tell me in July that too many cookies would make me sick? I personally didn't think that cookies ever made me sick. I couldn't figure out why eating a few extra cookies was such a big deal anyway. But I never could figure out *parents* either! Sometimes their rules just didn't make sense. Anyway, it was *eating* that first made me realize Clarence was gone.

I had just opened a box of Christmas cookies that were shaped and decorated like all sorts of animals. Each one wore a Santa hat, elf outfit, or reindeer antlers. I spotted a rather homely-looking mouse. It had mounds of icing on it which made it very tempting... but yuck! The thought of eating a mouse was just gross! My Dad had told me once about a friend of his that had bitten the head off a live mouse on account of being dared to do it. That always made me feel queasy about mice. But Clarence would love it! It would be fun to feed him bits of a mouse cookie. I grabbed another cookie for myself and went hunting my kitty friend.

I couldn't find him. He wasn't curled up in the pile of dirty laundry in my closet. He wasn't stalking the basement looking for live mice. He wasn't on top of the car in the garage. I looked under furniture, on top of furniture, even behind pictures on the wall. Like he would have been behind a picture! No Clarence! I went to the living room and asked Papa Bear. He simply looked knowingly out the window toward the street. I concluded that Clarence had gone wandering again. Well, I'd just have to save the cookie until he got back. I put the mouse cookie away and waited. By evening, Clarence still wasn't back. I was beginning to get a tiny bit worried. Clarence always came back at suppertime!

I didn't sleep well that night. Dad and Mom told me that for sure Clarence would be back in the morning. But how did they *know* that? I dreamed that I had been captured by sewer rats and made to eat mice and beans every day. It was a terrible nightmare! When morning came I stumbled over my slippered feet, racing down the steps, yelling for Clarence. Papa Bear looked me in the eye and looked out the window. I knew right away. Clarence was still gone!

Two dreadful days followed. I moped. Nobody could cheer me up. I concluded that Clarence was dead. I finally convinced my parents to help me look around the neighborhood. Like dutiful parents, they plodded along the snowy streets, stopping at each house to ask if they had seen our cat. Nobody had. I couldn't figure it out! A black cat with a white patch over his heart should have been easy to see against the snow. But no one had seen him. My parents said that probably something had happened to Clarence. Just yesterday, they *knew* he'd be back. Now they said he probably *wouldn't* be. Just one more time I couldn't figure them out!

I was miserable. I marched into the kitchen. On the counter I saw the mouse cookie staring at me. It made me angry. I slapped my hand down on it. Yuck! The gooey icing stuck between my fingers and the crumbs felt disgustingly crumbly! I washed the remains down the kitchen sink and thought more nasty thoughts about mice. After all, it probably was a mouse's fault. For sure Clarence had gone looking for mice and gotten hurt somehow. I decided I hated mice!

Christmas Eve didn't mean much to me that year. Usually I was crazy excited about Christmas and all the presents I would get. But that year, all I could think of was Clarence. I prayed for a miracle. My parents had taught me to pray. They said God cared about anything that bothers us and that He's always watching over us. They said nothing is too difficult for God. I wanted to have faith, *but what was faith anyway?* I felt angry that God hadn't brought my pet back to me yet. I figured if God was looking out for me, He'd know that I desperately needed Clarence.

By evening, I hit my lowest point of misery and despair. I threw myself on the sofa, buried my face in the cushion and cried. Big kids of 10 weren't supposed to cry much, but I couldn't help it! Clarence was gone... probably dead... never coming back! I cried until it seemed my tear bin had run dry. Then I just lay there feeling numb. I don't know how long it took me to know that I wasn't alone, but gradually I realized I was feeling something soft across the back of my neck. I lifted my head. It was Papa Bear. He had climbed down from the back of the sofa and was curled up right by my shoulder with his tail softly draped across my neck. Papa Bear! Why hadn't I thought of it before? Papa Bear could find Clarence. I knew he could!

I jumped up, almost flipping Papa Bear in a somersault from the sofa and ran for my Dad. It took some convincing because Dad wasn't at all sure that a cat had any bloodhound instincts, but he finally agreed to give it a try. We bundled up and headed out into the snow-covered streets... with Papa Bear leading the way, attached to us by a piece of tinsel I had grabbed off the tree to use as a leash!

Papa Bear circled the house several times. My hopes began to sag. Then, in that kingly way of his, he began strutting down the street. My hopes went up just a little bit. We reached an overturned garbage can and Papa Bear stopped to investigate. My hopes went

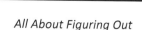

down. I scolded, reminding him that we were looking for Clarence. He immediately turned toward an alley. My hopes soared again. Papa Bear began to strain against the tinsel. He was actually moving fast. I had never seen Papa Bear move fast before! We were almost at the end of the alley when he stopped abruptly. I wasn't expecting it and tripped right over him, landed on a patch of ice and slid right into a stack of cardboard boxes that were leaning against the building. They came tumbling down, knocking me over and hitting my Dad on the head. But Papa Bear had managed to step speedily out of the way and was now standing a few yards away on the other side of the alley, his gaze fixed on an overturned crate.

I crawled over to see what he was looking at. It was already pretty dark outside and difficult to see. I carefully tipped the crate back. I leaned down close and squinted hard. I gasped! It was Clarence, all right... curled up and dreadfully motionless. He looked dead. But, in the dim moonlight, I could see the gentle rise and fall of his white patch. At least he was still breathing! I started to reach for him, then, startled I drew back. Something had moved and it wasn't Clarence! What was that beside him? Cautiously I leaned closer. There beside him, snuggled against his fur... I still can't get over it... beside him, nestled all cozy was a scrawny, little *mouse!*

My dad was amazed too! Of course, Papa Bear didn't look one bit surprised. Clarence opened one eye, but didn't seem to have the strength to even lift his head. He did move his paw just a bit... kind of curled it protectively around the sickly mouse. Obviously, Clarence was taking care of this creature! Dad grabbed one of the smaller cardboard boxes I had knocked over, put his wool scarf in the bottom and gently laid Clarence and the mouse in the bottom of the box. I couldn't believe it!

"Why are you taking the *mouse*?" I demanded. "Mom won't like this!" Actually, I didn't like the idea of taking a mouse home!

"If we hadn't come along, Clarence would probably have died within a few hours. He would have died trying to protect this little creature from freezing. We can't leave him behind." Was Dad making any sense?

As we headed home I looked up at the sky and saw the stars and remembered that this was Christmas. I shook my head. How a *cat* could take pity on a *mouse*... I would never understand. And how a big Daddy cat, that never left the house, could lead us to Clarence in a lonely alley, was mind-boggling. Had God done this? Was this a for-real miracle? I thought about the orange crate. It was kind of like a manger. Why *did* Jesus give up heaven to come to a dirty world? Why *did* He give up His own life for the very people that were his enemies? It was all pretty hard to understand.

All About Figuring Out

As you can imagine, that Christmas was extra special to me, one I'll never forget! That Christmas, I figured out that there are some things in life I would maybe never be able to figure out... things like cats, and parents and Jesus. Maybe some things were too special to figure out. Maybe I just needed to love them even if I didn't always understand them. And just maybe, I figured... that might be what faith is all about!

*Truly I tell you,
whatever you did for
one of the least of these
brothers and sisters of mine,
you did for me...
and whatever you did not do
for one of the least of these,
you did not do for me.*

Matthew 25:40, 45

Christmas Annie

I was only eleven at the time, but I learned a very important lesson on Christmas Eve, 1963. And it was all because of *Annie*...

Annie Lillie was just about the most stuck-up kid I ever knew. If medals had been given out for snobbery, she would have won gold, hands down! To my 7th grade mind she certainly didn't have much to be proud of. She was absolutely the scrawniest kid in all junior high. Everything about her was revoltingly thin! Her elbows were so pointy she could have registered them as lethal weapons. A jab from one of them could make even the 8th grade football star wince. Her hair was brown and straggly and the rest of us girls used to whisper behind her back, wondering if she washed it in Oil of *Uglay* shampoo! Even her voice was thin and squeaky with an edge to it that grated on all her classmates. But worst of all was her nose. She actually had a *skinny* nose! I'd never met anyone else with a skinny nose. Noses are supposed to be kind of round and cherry-like... they're supposed to fill up a decent amount of space on your face. But hers was so narrow it looked like an exclamation mark with two periods under it and, if you can

imagine, she managed to keep this skinny thing pointed up most of the time.

I guess Annie knew enough not to brag on her looks, but she bragged about almost everything else. She bragged about her brains and how she had been the "top English student" at Strathmore School (that was the snobby girls' school she had attended before moving to our neighborhood). And she even acted like she knew more than our English teacher! The scary thing is, I think maybe she did know more. But, to the rest of us 7th graders, that seemed strange and un-natural. Our teacher must have thought so too because she always acted a little jittery when Miss Lillie raised her hand to ask a question. The reason Annie probably knew so much was because her "fa-a-a-h-ther" (that's how she always pronounced it, with her nose in the air of course!) was a professor at Hillfield, another private snob school in the area. She quoted her "fa-a-a-h-ther" all the time, until we could hardly stand it. Nobody could be that smart, except God Himself and sometimes I think Annie actually believed her dad knew more than the Almighty!

Annie entered our lives for the first time in 7th grade. Maybe that was part of the problem. She just didn't fit in with all the rest of us junior highers. She hadn't grown up in our section of town or been part of our group of kids through the early grades. She had missed all the good stuff! She hadn't been there when Louie Katz ate an entire jar of paste in kindergarten. The teacher got so hysterical with panic that we got a whole extra recess while she and the principal and the school nurse tried to figure out what to tell his mother. We called him Gluey Louie from that time on.

Annie missed the time in 3rd grade when Helen Barjoutski flattened the 5th grade teacher, Mr. Crady. Helen had come flying out of the girls' restroom and nailed Mr. Crady, who was walking down the hall, smack in the middle of his forehead with the swinging wooden door. He was knocked out cold in the corridor, with a goose egg that was more like the size of an ostrich egg. He missed the rest of that day and all the next. Of course we loved having a day and a half with an inexperienced substitute!

And Annie never got to visit the city waste disposal plant with our fifth grade class and get awarded a genuine "sewage disposal of tomorrow" hat. They were the neatest hats! The whole class concocted a plan to bring them to school one day and just for a joke, when the noon warning bell rang, we would pull them out of our desks and put them on. We thought Miss Waterby would think we were pretty funny. How were we to know that on that particular day the mayor of the whole city was going to drop in unexpectedly on our classroom at exactly 30 seconds past the warning bell? Miss Waterby

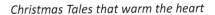

was mortified and kept trying to explain why we had these hats with a big commode design on the front of them! We never forgot that day.

Annie had missed all of that! She just didn't seem to be part of our lives. However, she kind of made herself part of my life, because I had the misfortune of having to walk right past her house on my way to and from school each day. For some unknown reason, she tried to attach herself to me. I sure as anything didn't know why. Oh, I was a Christian, so I knew I couldn't be outright rude to her like some of the kids, but I got as close to it as I dared without endangering my salvation! With my real friends, I would chatter and laugh and share about my life. With Annie, I mostly listened in bored silence while she bragged on and on about her house or her brains or her "fa-a-a-h-ther!"

One day she pulled a real fast one on me. It's the same trick some guys play on girls when they ask them for a date. They call and say, "Are you doing anything Friday night?" If you ask me, that's really playing dirty. Because if you can't think of something you're doing, he's got you pinned for the next question ... "Well in that case, would you go out with me?" Then if you say, "No," it's like saying that an evening with him is worse than doing nothing on a Friday night! That sounds pretty mean. So he has you trapped into saying you'll go.

Anyway, that's what Annie did one day on the way home from school. She asked, "Hey, are you doing anything after school tomorrow afternoon?" She really caught me off guard. I closed one eye and, with the other, tried to search the sky for some answer. I began stammering. I hoped desperately that God would do a miracle and fill my mouth with a good answer like, "Well, actually I've been planning to help out at the city rescue mission tomorrow afternoon, serving meals to the homeless... sorry Annie." But the Lord didn't give me such a brainwave and so she took my umms and uhhs as a "Nothing." Shc had me! To my horror she announced that since I had nowhere else to be, she would expect me to come to her house after school the next day to listen to a long play recording of Shakespeare's Macbeth!

Don't get me wrong, I kind of liked Shakespeare... he wasn't the bad part. The terrible thing was that kids might see me going into Annie Lillie's house and conclude that I liked her. Even if they didn't see us, I knew she'd brag about it to everyone the following day at school. And then the whole school would find out! I would be labeled Annie's friend. Could anything be worse than that? I didn't think so. Why, this could ruin my testimony. Lots of kids knew that I claimed to be a Christian. But if they thought I liked Annie Lillie, they'd probably reject me and my God. Plus, this could be really damaging to my reputation! Kids might start to

think I was stuck up too. Then they might talk about me behind my back, just like they did about Annie... just like I myself often did about Annie.

That whole evening I tried so hard to think up some excuse not to go. I couldn't come up with any, except an outright lie. Unfortunately that would be sinning and I certainly didn't want to commit sin because of her. Although I was tempted! I prayed to be overtaken with sickness so I could legitimately beg off. Wouldn't you know it? God kept me healthy all night long.

School the next day was horrible. Annie bragged to everybody that I was going to her house that afternoon. I was sure every single class member was looking at me like I had lost a screw in my brain or something. Kids that usually hung around with me at lunch period huddled on the other side of the classroom, whispering and looking my way. I decided I hated Annie Lillie!

It seemed I had no choice but to go through with the ordeal. But I did not have to like it! So like a martyr going to the guillotine, I accompanied Annie to her house after school. I was quiet and cold and aloof the whole time. I asked to see the script that went along with the recording, curled up on a chair and pretended to be following along with the record. When she would try to make one of her know-it-all comments, I'd tap the booklet and shake my finger, to make it look like I was

really engrossed in the dialogue. Actually, I was count-
ing the minutes until it would be over and I could go
home! I escaped just as soon as I could, thanking her in
a not-very-sincere tone of voice.

The next day was the last school day before
Christmas vacation. Of course Annie blabbed all day
long about the wonderful time I had at her house!
Classmates gawked at me with strange expressions on
their faces. I figured the only hope I had of regaining my
social standing was if kids would forget all about this
over Christmas break. Maybe after the holidays I could
recover my damaged reputation.

That afternoon I tried to hurry out of the school
without Annie spotting me. No such luck! She caught up to
me and grabbed me by my scarf. She about strangled me!

"Wait a minute!" she panted. "I want to ask you
something."

"Oh no!" I shuddered to myself. "She's going to try
to get me to spend more time with her. This is really
getting awful!"

"So what do you want?" I asked quite impatiently,
without bothering to turn around and face her.

She must have slowed down and stopped in the
middle of the sidewalk. When she didn't answer me, I
shrugged disgustedly and turned to look at her. I was

stunned! For once, her skinny nose was pointed down and two big tears were rolling down her cheeks. What was wrong with Annie... Miss always-in-control-always-Miss-Perfect Annie?

"Annie, what's wrong? Are you okay?" I even managed something close to concern in my voice.

"Why doesn't *anybody* like me?" she blurted out. "Everyone hates me... you hate me, all the other kids hate me! *I* don't even like me!"

I couldn't think of anything to say. All of a sudden I felt sorry for her. Why, Annie wasn't so in love with herself after all. This girl actually had feelings. I thought about how we had all rejected her so often.

"Annie," I finally began, but she shoved me out of the way and ran past. "Annie," I called after her, but she wouldn't stop or look back. I heard her muffled sobs as she ran away and I was left standing alone on the sidewalk with big fluffy snowflakes beginning to land on my eyelids. I blinked them away. I wouldn't want anyone to think I was crying about Annie... because I wasn't.

It was hard to get Annie out of my mind. Funny how someone I had always tried not to think about was now the main subject of my thoughts. I told myself to quit thinking about her...because the next day was Christmas Eve. There would be a big program at church and I had a part. This year someone had decided to let a few girls bc shepherds (females had never been shepherds before) and some of us junior high girls had volunteered. I was determined to stop worrying about Annie. Who cared about her anyway? I focused my attention on the upcoming program.

The night of the pageant was cold and snowy... just like Christmas weather should be. All the kids and Sunday School teachers were rushing around, tripping over too-long bathrobes, straightening crooked coat-hanger halos and locating lost gold, frankincense and myrrh. After the usual hustle and bustle, everyone was finally in place, nervously ready to act out the story of Jesus' birth.

The moment arrived when we shepherds climbed the steps of the platform and took our places out in the lonely fields (stage left, actually). The spotlights were glaring. My costume was hot enough by itself but, besides that, the whole church was roasting because of being packed with so many people. I was sweating up a storm. When the angel of the Lord appeared I thought I might faint dead away from heat exhaustion! What a realistic portrayal that would have been. But I managed to hang onto consciousness and then ran with the other shepherds to the stable in Bethlehem. This journey was actually just six steps across to the other side of the platform but, considering we had to weave through and

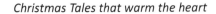

step over all the nursery kids who were dressed as tiny angels and arranged across the middle of the stage, it did take a while to arrive at the manger. Finally, we were there and I was the first shepherd to kneel in front of the wooden box filled with hay. I couldn't see over the top of the manger but I knew there was supposed to be a real live baby in there. I'd heard that the pastor and his wife had offered their own newborn to play the part of baby Jesus. I'd never even seen their kid yet. This was a real young one ... perfect for the part. Well, not exactly perfect. Their baby was actually a girl but I guess they figured, if they wrapped her in a blue blanket, nobody would be able to tell the difference.

The atmosphere was quite wonderful, really! The audience was hushed. Mary looked peaceful and dreamy. Joseph looked contented and kind. The choir was humming Silent Night softly in the background. Everyone was caught up in the drama. I let myself imagine I was actually there in Bethlehem, about to get a first glimpse at the One who was sent to be the Messiah of the world... my Savior! I dared to raise myself up just a bit so I could peek over the edge of the manger and get a glimpse of the sleeping baby Jesus. I was breathless with the emotion of the moment!

I peered down into the manger to see the precious babe... and I jerked back in shocked surprise. I'll never forget that sight!

The infant was there all right, and looking right at me. But all I saw was... that baby's *nose!* It was skinny. *Skinny!* Not a cute, chubby, button baby nose like most newborns have, but thin and bony and... you guessed it... *pointed up!* I looked in the manger to see Jesus but instead all I could see was... Annie! Two big tears slid out of my eyes and dropped on the hay. Some long-ago-memorized Bible verses suddenly popped into my mind. *I tell you the truth, whatever you did for one of the least of these brothers and sisters of mine, you did for me... and whatever you did not do for one of the least of these, you did not do for me* (Matthew 25:40, 45).

There by the manger I knew that, in rejecting Annie, I had been rejecting Jesus. *Jesus!* The Savior I claimed to love and serve! There by the manger I saw Annie in a new light... she was someone Jesus would love, even with all her bragging and obnoxious habits, even with all her covered-up insecurity and fear. There by the manger I began to love Annie. And there by the manger I learned that Christmas is not just for you and me but Christmas is for all the Annies in this world!

I'll never forget that night. Nor will I forget Annie who became my friend and helped me learn to look past noses to needs, past people's behavior to the Savior who loves them, and past my own pride to a world that needs Jesus! *Thank God for Annie!*

The Word became flesh
and made his dwelling among us.
We have seen his glory,
the glory of the one and only Son,
who came from the Father,
full of grace and truth.

John 1:14

The Other Side of the Fence

The year I turned 12, my parents got the crazy idea to go south for Christmas. And when I say south, I'm not talking about Florida or Texas. Those places would have been bad enough. No, they wanted something more exotic and tropical. How they decided on Trinidad I have no idea. They never even asked my opinion or considered me... the one they called their "Princess!" Now that I was almost a teenager, I should at least have been consulted... especially since it meant changing our normal Christmas activities. But no... Dad and Mom simply announced their plan and expected me to not make a fuss.

Oh, but I did fuss. And a lot! I didn't like their idea one bit! Christmas without cold weather and snow? Christmas without going to the tree farm to find and chop down our own perfect tree? Christmas without our house decorated from top to bottom, inside and out? How could we miss Grandma's home-cooked turkey dinner? And... *the cookies!* How could we enjoy the holidays without *those cookies?*

Then Dad and Mom dropped an even bigger bombshell: this vacation was supposed to count

as everybody's Christmas gift! What? No presents? Unimaginable! I thought Christmas was supposed to be about family and traditions. My parents were messing things up big time. How dare they?

Mom acted really dreamy about it all. She'd take these big, deep sighs and talk in a strange, sing-song-y voice... "Just think... ten days of blue skies, warm sunshine, no baking, cooking, decorating... pure relaxation. What a heavenly Christmas this will be!" Was she losing her mind? I thought I'd heard something about women her age becoming unreasonable. I concluded this must be her problem and that trying to debate the issue with her would be pointless.

My older siblings were ecstatic about the whole idea and immediately began shopping for flowered shorts, orange flip-flops and sun-tan lotion. Why couldn't they stick up for me on this?

So I went to Dad and pleaded with him to reconsider. I reminded him that we would miss the annual Christmas pageant at church. Wasn't that something *all* Christian families participated in? "Dad, I think you're forgetting the real *spiritual* significance of Christmas. I thought that was important to you! But if you take our family to Trinidad, it's obvious you don't really care about God!" I put on my best expression of shocked disbelief. Maybe I could guilt him into staying home. To be honest, I knew I wouldn't actually miss the Christmas pageant at all. I had heard that my Sunday School class was going to have to dress up like sheep, cows and donkeys. I didn't relish the idea of wearing a ridiculous, stifling hot costume and crawling around saying, "baa," or, "moo," or, worse yet, "hee-haw." How humiliating! Going to Trinidad would actually rescue me from that. Nevertheless I was willing to endure being a bull or an a-... excuse me... a *donkey*, if that would keep us home for Christmas.

Dad was not moved by my logic. He matter-of-factly explained that he had been under a great deal of stress lately and a vacation would do him good. Plus the idea of not having to shovel snow appealed to him a whole lot. But I liked snow! What about *me? Didn't anyone care about me?*

I guessed not because, on December 16, I found myself on an airplane headed to Trinidad. I had actually considered trying to lose my family in the airport and imagined myself spending Christmas at home alone... just like in the movie. Then my family would be sorry! But I think they must have read my mind, because they never let me out of their sight. They escorted me, like a prisoner in chains, to seat 17A. What a horrible Christmas this was going to be!

As the plane took off, I pressed my face against the window and said a silent mournful good-bye to cold and snow and Christmas. Then I stubbornly folded my arms, put my head back against the head-rest, closed my eyes and refused to look out the window again... even when the rest of the family started "oohing" and "aahing" over sparkling blue water, cloudless sky and dazzling white beaches.

Their maddening "ooh's" and "aah's" just kept coming, right through our landing, the taxi ride through town and arrival at the sprawling resort hotel, just one block from the beach. But I stubbornly kept my gaze straight ahead. I didn't care about the sights and sounds of Trinidad!

Once at the hotel, I had to admit that our room was huge and luxurious with an awesome view of the ocean. But it just wasn't *Christmas-y!* How could my family enjoy all of this when I was so miserable? Didn't they care one bit about my feelings?

I didn't have to ponder that question long because soon after settling into our room my Dad took me into the bathroom to have a private talk. He sat me on the edge of the tub and he plunked on the pot (closed lid of course). I figured I was in trouble and tried to quickly side-track him by asking what that other funny-looking pot was for. He said, "Ask your mother." He then proceeded to give a stern lecture about choosing to be happy, even when we don't feel like it. He said, "Princess... there are lots of times in life when we need to do things we don't want to do. We can gripe and complain which only makes us miserable and everyone around us as well, or we can choose to put a smile on our face and decide to be cheerful. I know you are disappointed about missing Christmas at home, but I believe the Lord wants you to make an effort to enjoy our time here."

Why'd he have to bring God into this conversation? Now he was trying to guilt me! But I knew my Dad. Although he was telling me I had a choice, he was using his "you-don't-really have-any-choice-in-this-matter" tone of voice. He ended up with, "I know you'll choose to have a good time with the rest of us." Before I could stamp my foot or pout or anything, he got off the pot and walked out.

"Well," I thought, "I guess I have to *act* pleasant, but that doesn't mean I have to *like* the situation." I decided I would put on a good front but, when the vacation was over, I'd let them know what a miserable time I'd really had and how they had forced me to endure it like a martyr. I'd guilt them all!

So I jumped the ocean waves. I swam in the hotel pool. I created some incredible-in-my-opinion sand sculptures. At mealtimes I devoured shrimp and lobster and some truly scrumptious Trinidadian pastries called,

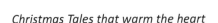

"doubles." But always, just below the surface of my actions was an ache that wouldn't go away. This wasn't bad for a vacation, but it wasn't *Christmas!*

One afternoon, as the rest of my family lounged around the pool, I wandered over to a grove of palm trees and poinsettia bushes along the white-washed solid fence that bordered the sides and back of the whole hotel property. At least poinsettias were Christmas-y. And I could pretend the white fence was a mountain of snow. I noticed several small holes in the fence... knotholes that had popped clean through the wood and of course my 12-year-old's curiosity couldn't wait to spy on the world outside.

I chose one of the larger holes, large enough to fit my hand through, certainly large enough to look through. When I squatted down it was at perfect eye-level. I pressed my face against the wood and peered through the opening. I couldn't believe what I saw!

Right smack up against the fence was a ... what would you call it? A hut? A shack? Those words seemed too fancy. Several crooked poles held up some sheets of cardboard and an occasional piece of aluminum. There were no walls except for the hotel fence which served as the back wall. There were several ragged blankets here and there on the dirt floor. A naked dark-skinned toddler lay fast asleep on one of the blankets, while flies buzzed around his face. In the center was a wobbly-looking stove-type contraption that had a single dented cooking pot on top. A pleasant-looking (although very poorly-dressed) young woman stirred something in the pot. There was a smoldering flame in the wood below. Could she be making supper? Near her a man sat on the only chair. He had an old board on his lap and was cleaning a fish with a little pocket-knife. He whistled while he worked. Would that be their main course? A few crates scattered here and there appeared to contain some clothes, personal items, a sack of rice, and an assortment of mismatched dishes and utensils. Over in the corner was a rusty wash tub. Above it a few tattered and stained garments hung from a make-shift wash line. A girl about my age was scrubbing clothes in the tub. She wore shorts and flip-flops. Her shirt had so many holes, she might as well not have been wearing it! She hummed cheerfully as she worked. Where did she get the water? There was no faucet. Of course not. There wasn't even a sink! A younger boy, similarly dressed, sat in the dirt on the other side of the shelter, pushing a stick around and making happy "boy-sounds." Two chickens scratched the dirt and clucked beside him.

I could see that beyond this shelter were many other similar structures... a whole village of poverty. Mangy dogs and cats roamed everywhere; wheelbarrow-type carts rattled by, pushed by young boys. Old men with black teeth sat around like beggars. Old women threw

dirty water into a gutter. My parents had described such places to me and missionaries at church had showed some pictures, but nothing... nothing I'd seen or heard about before compared to this! I felt like I could hardly breathe. The disgusting odor I'd caught a whiff of only made matters worse. I turned away and tried to stifle a cough.

When I looked back, the girl was looking right at me. I was embarrassed to be caught spying, but she gave me a huge grin and I thought, "Wow, this girl is really beautiful, although someone should give her a decent shirt!" She quickly slung the last piece of laundry over the line and came over to a crate near the fence. She rummaged for a moment and then came right over to my hole. I backed up a bit as her brown arm came through, hand outstretched. On her palm was a piece of candy. The paper wrapping was almost worn off in some places and appeared stuck fast in others. It was the kind of thing my mother would have looked at and said, "Don't touch that! It's dirty!" But this was obviously a gesture of kindness and I shyly reached out and took it. "Thanks!" I said. I didn't have a candy to give her, so I quickly pulled a poinsettia off the bush behind me (hoping the hotel security hadn't seen me) and shoved it through the fence. She smiled, thanked me and promptly stuck it behind her ear. "Girls are girls everywhere!" I thought.

And so began a daily ritual of gift-giving. I gave her a banana I had sneaked from the hotel breakfast buffet, a Mars bar I'd forgotten about in my carry-on suitcase, a complimentary bottle of lotion left in our hotel room by the maid service, and finally, my favorite pink T-shirt with butterflies on it. She gave me a chipped marble, a piece of cardboard with a happy face drawn on it (looked like she had used charred wood to do the sketch), a straggly hair ribbon, and what was probably most dear to her... a coin. I felt like my gifts were cheap compared to hers. Every gift I gave was easy. There were lots more where they came from. Why... I had more clothes in my suitcase than her whole family owned! Every gift she gave seemed priceless. Each was a sacrifice, a true offering of love.

I couldn't get over that she and her family seemed so cheerful and content in spite of their miserable surroundings. We talked and laughed... I loved her British-sounding accent. In four short days, we became best friends!

I had to miss seeing her on Christmas Eve, because my parents insisted we attend a church service. Every-one seemed to find the service wonderful, except me. Honestly, the tropical version of the Christmas story left me cold... well, hot, actually. Then there was the big hotel feast that went late into the night. Christmas morning, all my family wanted to do was "veg" by the

pool. That was fine with me. I couldn't wait to kneel by the fence and visit with my friend. I had been racking my brains to come up with a truly perfect Christmas gift for her. This would be our final day together. What could I give her that would be extra-special? I actually prayed about it and, although I didn't hear a voice speaking or see a neon sign flashing, I knew God gave me a great idea.

I looked through the hole. Her family was there as usual, but not busy at work like they had been every other day. Today my friend's young mother lay peacefully asleep on one of the blankets with her husband snoring softly beside her. The naked toddler crawled around in the dirt and her brother was keeping him from getting too close to the fire. My friend sat by the fire with a bundle of laundry in her arms. "No holiday for her," I thought. But I was happy to see she was wearing my pink T-shirt.

I coughed and stuck my hand through the hole. For once, I was going to give my gift first! She looked up and gave me the biggest grin ever. Setting the laundry down, she came over to the fence. I held out my gift. I had wrapped it in a piece of hotel stationery, tied with a toilet paper bow (I was trying to be more resourceful like she was). She took it, unwrapped it and gently touched the heart-shaped locket my parents had given me the day I asked Jesus to be my Savior and Lord of my life. I reached out my finger and pushed the little button that

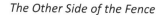

opened the locket. On the inside was a picture of a cross and a simple verse... I wasn't sure she could read, so I read the words for her..."We love Him, because He first loved us."

"I know." She nodded and smiled. "I know Jesus too." I was thrilled to discover that she was a Christian. And then I realized that this girl who hummed while she scrubbed and gave when it cost, knew Christ in a way I didn't. I envied her.

Suddenly her expression changed. She hung her head. "I am so sorry. I have no gift for you today," she said. "There has been much happening in my family." For a split second I was disappointed. Not even a gift from my best friend on Christmas. And then I heard a strange sound coming from... where? I thought it came from the pile of rags she'd left by the fire.

My friend turned immediately and rushed over to pick up the crying bundle. She walked back to the fence with her newborn baby brother cradled in her arms. "He come last night. Just like Jesus. Would you like to touch him?"

I reached out and touched the tiny hand of the baby in the slum. He stopped crying. "Look, he likes you," my friend said. I looked at the infant and then I surveyed his home. Dirt floors, tattered shreds of cloth, practically nothing to eat, flies, chickens, and mangy dogs. I smelled the garbage and the urine. I felt the

hopelessness of it all. *"And the Word became flesh and dwelt among us."* The Christmas pageant words flashed through my mind. Who would choose to be born into this? Who, but the God of the universe that loved us so much He would do anything to reach out to us... even if it meant climbing the fence between a perfect heaven and a filthy earth.

And then I thought about my selfishness and stubbornness, my anger and complaining. I had my own stinking shack. It was inside of me. But God loved me enough to enter that slum too and He was even willing to clean it up... when I let Him. Suddenly Christmas was clearer to me than it had ever been before.

I took my friend's hand and pulled it through the fence. I kissed it gently and whispered, "Good-bye. Thank you for all your gifts. You gave me more than you'll ever know. I'll never forget you!" Wiping a tear from my cheek I got up from my knees and turned around.

Dad was standing right there. "Found a hole in the fence, did ya?" he asked.

"Yeah," I replied. I wondered how long he'd been standing there.

"Anything of interest over there?" he continued.

"Yeah." I lifted up my arms to him and he reached down to me. We wrapped each other in a big hug. I

whispered tearfully in his ear, "Thanks Dad, for bringing me here. This has been the best Christmas ever!"

"Really, Princess?" he responded gently. "I'm very glad to hear that. I've been praying that it would turn out to be *extra* special for you."

"Well, your prayer was answered, Dad. It's been *really* extra special! Even without snow and decorations and..."

"Grandma's cookies?" he asked.

"Yeah, even without Grandma's cookies." We both laughed and then walked hand-in-hand back to the hotel.

Hours later, I had my nose pressed once again against an airplane window. Dad leaned over to me and whispered in my ear. "By the way," he asked, "I'm curious. What exactly did you see through that hole?"

I was quiet for a few moments. I thought about my friend and her sacrificial gifts. I recalled her family's joy even in the midst of such tough surroundings. I pictured the beautiful baby born in the slum. I remembered how my eyes were opened to a world outside my own. I wondered again at the incredible love of a Savior who would give up heaven... just to live in... *me!* "Why Dad... it should be obvious," I announced with a twinkle in my eye. "What did I see? Why of course I'll tell you what I saw. I saw... *the other side of the fence!*"

But when the right time came,
the time God decided on,
he sent his Son,
born of a woman,
born as a Jew,
to buy freedom for us...

Galatians 4:4-5 (TLB)

Timing is Everything

When leaves on the Main Street trees began turning yellow, I knew autumn was coming. So December wasn't far off. And that meant it was time for me to start formulating my Christmas *wish list!* The list I made when I was eleven proved to be one I would never forget.

Each fall weekend of 1990 I grabbed the bunch of ads that made the Sunday newspaper so fat. I disappeared with them to my bedroom where I was growing a stack of catalogs. It seemed like new ones arrived in the mail every day and my mother would have thrown them all in the trash if I hadn't rescued them and added them to the stash by my bed.

At night I'd hop into bed and examine every colorful page of tantalizing items... clothing, toys, jewelry, books, movies, TV's and stereos, candy, sporting equipment, even décor for a growing girl's bedroom. As a soon-to-be adolescent, I was fascinated with all these things. Funny, I could remember when I only looked at the pictures of toys and candy. I guess growing up was expanding my interests. It would be hard to narrow down my wants to just a few items. But I knew that I had to be reason-

able. After all, my parents were not millionaires. I would pore over those catalogs until I was almost falling asleep. Then I would go through the nightly ritual of Bible reading and memorized prayer that my parents had drilled into me when I was just a little girl. The words I read and said really didn't mean much to me... except that I figured they kept me on the good side of God.

Years ago... when I was only seven... my older brother had scolded me for making such a long list of things I wanted for Christmas.

"Em," he began (my real name, Emma Lynn had been cut to this shorter, easier version when I was still a toddler), "let me see your list." I handed over the paper on which I had carefully copied the names of 54 objects I had picked out for my parents to give me for Christmas. "This list is ridiculous!" he chided. He produced a calculator and began adding up the prices of each item. "Em," and this time he sounded disgusted, "if Dad and Mom bought you everything on your list, it would cost them three thousand, four hundred and sixty-three dollars and seventy-seven cents! Are you crazy? They don't have that kind of money!"

Of course he was right. I had been silly. So I narrowed my list to only 40 wishes, and proudly showed my brother what I had accomplished. He just shook his head and rolled his eyes. "You're hopeless," I heard him

mutter as he handed back my precious document and walked away.

Four years later, I was much older and wiser. I had gained a greater understanding of money, prices, budgets, et cetera and so, after many agonizing hours studying the ads and catalogs, I had finally decided on the one... yes, that's right... just *one* item I desired for Christmas! It was beautiful and, although it cost more than any single gift I had ever received in the past, I figured my parents could afford it.

The catalog description read like this... "A sleek silver dial shines brilliantly against the white mother-of-pearl face. The sapphire crystal provides superior scratch resistance. Also featured is a solar-powered quartz movement so it never needs a battery. Water resistant to 30 meters. Stylish semi-circle stainless steel links complete the amazing look. This is a stunning timepiece you will treasure for years."

For my eighth birthday, I had received a watch. It had a pink, patent leather wristband and there was a picture of a ballerina in a pink fluffy tutu on its face. Instead of a second hand, the ballerina's knees bent and straightened with each tick. I had been quite delighted with it when I was eight but, for a going-on-twelve-year-old, it seemed way too childish. Besides, the ballerina had quit dancing some time ago and was frozen in

a very unbecoming position. The patent leather was cracked, most of the pink shine had flaked off and it had a smell that resembled the odor of belly-button lint mixed with my brother's stinky gym socks. Only generous applications of baby powder made it bearable.

My parents had always said that I had good taste and that I was mature for my age. I was confident they would be impressed with my choice of watch. Mom would like the appearance and my technology-addicted Dad would love the no-battery-needed feature. I liked the water resistant part, even though I had no idea how deep thirty meters was. I carefully tore the page, with the picture and description of my choice, out of the catalog, circled and starred the watch of my dreams and taped the ad to the refrigerator. All that was left was the waiting. There was just one month remaining until Christmas Day!

December is such a crazy month. There is always so much to do that the days seem to fly by. Each year I found myself enjoying the preparations more... the decorating, baking, gift-buying, the concerts, parties and family get-togethers. My older brother was doing a year of college studies in Europe, so he wouldn't be around for Christmas. That seemed strange and I missed him a lot but, even so, I was having great fun helping Mom with holiday prep. In the back of my mind, there was always the vision of that fabulous watch. I could picture it on my wrist. I could imagine the "oohs" and "aahs" from my friends when I returned to school on January 3rd with it gleaming on my arm. When the ad on the refrigerator disappeared, I was certain my parents had taken the bait.

As each day passed, I was regularly interrupted from my daydreams by my mother who seemed to have a never-ending list of jobs she wanted me to do. Three days before Christmas she came to me with yet another assignment.

"I need you to mail a letter for me, Em," she began and handed me a white business-size envelope, already sealed and stamped, with our church's return address in the top left corner. "This is very important. It needs to get in today's mail." As volunteer parish secretary-treasurer, she was always working on church business at home. This was evidently related to that.

"Sure," I replied eagerly. The post office was about a ten-minute walk from my house... three blocks up the street, past the school and playground, across the street at the traffic light beyond the school and then five buildings north on King Street. Although I was permitted to walk alone to and from school every day, I had never been allowed to go by myself as far as the post office. I'd been there many times with a parent or sibling, so I certainly knew the way. "She finally realizes how grown

up I am," I thought smugly. Grabbing my jacket and scarf and clutching the important envelope, I headed out the door.

It was an especially mild day for late December. A coat of melting snow hid the lawns, but the pavement was dry. As I approached the school, I spotted a group of my friends shooting baskets on the playground. "Hey Em," one of them shouted, "Come on over!"

I checked the ballerina on my wrist. No problem. The post office wouldn't close for a few more hours. Besides, I had been working so hard all that week. I thought I should be able to have a little fun. I deserved it. So I stuffed the letter in my pocket and ran to join the gang.

I really don't know how much time elapsed while we played several games of "Knock Out," "Around the World," and "Horse." But I made it to the post office just before closing and returned home again, without my mother even beginning to worry about my absence. As it turned out, I was the one who should have been worrying!

Christmas Eve, which happened to fall on a Sunday that year, arrived and I was almost bursting with excitement. Instead of a normal morning worship service, our church planned to hold a candlelight Christmas Eve service at 8 p.m. All morning I wandered around the house singing "Joy to the World," and every other

Christmas carol I could think of. I was especially elated because I had sneaked a peek at the gifts under the tree and spotted a small, rectangular one, wrapped in glittering foil paper, and tagged for me. It had to be my watch! I couldn't help but chuckle triumphantly!

After lunch my mother summoned me to the kitchen to give her a hand with some last-minute baking, in preparation for the wonderful feast we would devour the next day.

As we worked, Mom was also smiling and humming. She had that cat-that-just-swallowed-a-mouse kind of grin. In the middle of rolling out a section of pie dough, she sighed contentedly. "You know what, Em? It really is true what the Bible says!"

I rolled my eyes and thought sarcastically, "Isn't that what you've been drilling into me as long as I've existed?" Aloud I asked, "What do you mean?"

"Well, you know the Lakhdar family." Of course I knew them. Everybody at church knew them. They were the ongoing prayer request at every meeting in recent weeks. I couldn't believe how one family could have so much trouble. Just around the time I was beginning my Christmas list planning, they had moved to our city from one of those "I" countries in the Middle East... Iraq, Iran, Irabia... I couldn't remember which. They had no family in the U.S. and I gathered from some of the

know-everything-about-everybody old ladies at church, that most of their relatives back in their homeland were dead. The tiny little mother who always wore a black head-scarf had just been diagnosed with some kind of cancer and about a month back, the father had lost his job. Their dark-haired, olive-skinned thirteen-year-old daughter, Alayna, was gorgeous. I would have been jealous of her except that she always looked so pitifully sad and scared.

"What about them?" I asked.

"Some of us at the church office got to talking about them. The pastor said he knew they didn't have money to pay their rent which was due yesterday and they weren't going to have any gifts or nice meal on Christmas, because they simply had no money. So we took up a collection just among the staff and came up with enough cash for them to be able to pay their rent and buy some decent gifts and all the groceries they'd need for a special holiday meal. In fact, I wrote out the check and that's what was in the envelope you mailed for me on Friday. I called the post office. They assured me that if the letter got in Friday's mail it would be delivered to the Lakhdar's neighborhood early yesterday morning... just in time for them to drop off payment to their landlord and still get to some stores to buy gifts and food. Jesus said there is greater joy in giving than in receiving. Giving to the Lakhdar's has made me feel so very, very happy. I think this is the first time in my life that I really understand what Jesus meant."

I barely heard those last couple of sentences because, when Mom mentioned the post office's promise, I was suddenly filled with a very ominous dread. I remembered the sign above the mail slot... "Last mail pick-up for the day: 3:30 p.m." I had mailed Mom's envelope around 4:30 p.m. Friday. That meant it missed Friday's pick-up and would have waited until Saturday. There was no mail delivery Sunday and of course not on Monday either because that would be Christmas Day. The dark feeling was quickly turning into a sick one. The time I had spent playing with my friends would ruin Christmas for the Lakhdars. And if I confessed to my mother, I knew she'd lose her joy pretty quickly... not to mention the trouble I'd be making for myself! "Better just one of us should be miserable," I concluded. I continued spooning pumpkin mixture into the pastry. But only Mom kept on singing.

The sanctuary was beautiful that evening. Poinsettias lined the altar, pine boughs and softly-glowing candles filled the deep windowsills. Stretched across the rear of the platform was a Bethlehem street scene

beneath a starry sky. A rustic-looking stable and rough-hewn manger took center stage. Normally I would have been ecstatic...caught up in the dreamy silent-night mood. But that evening, sandwiched between my parents on a front pew, all I could think of was the envelope I had mailed late and the sad consequences that action would undoubtedly cause for a needy family. My awful secret nagged at my insides.

It didn't help when everyone turned to see Mary and Joseph walking down the center aisle. I almost gasped out loud. Alayna Lakhdar was Mary! Of course... she was the perfect choice. The real Mary had probably looked exactly like Alayna... young, dark, lovely, yet harboring a certain sadness others just didn't understand. I dropped my eyes. I couldn't keep looking at this girl I had wronged. I tried convincing myself that since she didn't know about the money, I didn't have to feel so bad. But guilt hounded me.

The deep booming voice of the pastor startled me back to the nativity scene as he narrated, "But when the *right time* came, the time God decided on, he sent his Son, born of a woman, born as a Jew, to buy freedom for us who were slaves to the law so that he could adopt us as his very own sons..."

The right time...*the right time!* If only I'd done what I was asked to do at the right time.

The pre-school angels with their crooked tinsel halos appeared and sang off-pitch glorias to third-grade shepherds in multi-colored kimonos. Then the pastor continued, "The shepherds said one to another, 'Let us now go even unto Bethlehem, and see this thing which is come to pass which the Lord hath made known unto us.'"

Let us now go... let us *now* go! I couldn't help but imagine how differently the whole Christmas story would have turned out had the characters delayed in carrying out God's instructions. What if Joseph and Mary had taken a little side trip on their way to Bethlehem? Would she have ended up giving birth, not in David's royal city as was prophesied, but in some other insignificant Israeli city? What if the shepherds had decided to go back to sleep or talk it over for a while? Would they have missed the baby in the manger completely? What if the wise men had parked their camels in Jerusalem for a few extra days? Would they have lost sight of the star and never found the infant Messiah? What if Joseph hadn't fled with his family to Egypt when God told him to get up and go? I shivered. That would have been disastrous.

I looked back at the stage. Beautiful Alayna, gently rocking baby Jesus, was surrounded by angels, shepherds, and wise men, all kneeling in worship of the newborn King. The pastor began his closing challenge... a clearer-than-I'd-ever-heard-before explanation of God's wonderful salvation plan… salvation made possible by the baby born to die for the sins of the world. For the first time it seemed to make sense because for the first time I realized I was one girl who needed saving!

"Behold, *now* is the accepted time; behold, *now* is the day of salvation." It seemed it wasn't the preacher's voice I heard, but God's. He was speaking to me! I'd heard His voice many times before, but always managed to ignore it. I figured I'd wait 'til I got older or felt more spiritual or had nothing better to do, to really connect with Him. Tears slid down my cheeks. I knew He was calling me to Himself … and this time I wouldn't wait a moment longer!

I'm so glad I didn't wait that Christmas Eve to commit my life to Jesus Christ. I've found that obeying Him… *immediately*… is by far the very best way to live.

But I made a second important decision that Christmas Eve. Following the close of the service, gulping back sobs of remorse, I confessed my post office transgression to my mom. She sighed the motherly sigh that says, "What in the world should I do with you now?" But then I whispered in her ear and then she whispered in my father's ear. And then they both smiled and said in unison, "Agreed!"

We hurried home and worked as a team to remove all the gift tags from the presents under our tree, replacing them with new tags made out to a family that needed them much more than we did. Early Christmas morning we loaded up the car with the new-named gifts, a bunch of decorations and a complete yuletide feast. Off we went to bless Alayna and her parents with the best Christmas we could give them.

Yes. Alayna got my watch... the one and only item on my wish list... and it looked lovely on her slender arm. I "oohed" and "aahed" over it and surprisingly felt enormously happy.

One day, months later, when I glanced at the aging pink ballerina on my wrist, it occurred to me that the Lakhdar family made out pretty good from my wrong-doing. After all, they got very nice gifts, a scrumptious meal and they still got the generous check in the mail on Tuesday.

Perhaps it wasn't late after all.

Now faith is confidence
in what we hope for
and assurance about
what we do not see.

Hebrews 11:1

More Than
a Sparrow

Jerome T. Jones, better known as JT was one
puzzled seven-year-old. Sitting cross-legged on
his bed, JT wondered what could be making his
parents so unhappy. Daddy seemed grouchy these days
and Mommy hardly ever smiled. This was supposed
to be an extra-happy time of year. December 25 was
only a couple of weeks away. He'd been crossing off the
days on his calendar. But so far his parents had hardly
mentioned the upcoming holiday.

He rubbed his head, totally messing up his rust-red
hair. Looking over at the birdcage beside his bed he
asked, "Jasper, what d'ya think is goin' on with Daddy
and Mommy?" Jasper was his pet house sparrow,
inherited from his Grandma Jones who had died only
a few months ago. She had found the baby bird on the
ground under her bird feeder last spring. Together, JT
and Grandma had fed and cared for the little orphan.
Now he was healthy and strong and was JT's best pal.
Daddy said Jasper's non-stop chirr-upping "bout drives
me crazy!" Mommy said, "If that bird ever poops on
my new Berber carpet when he's flying all around the
house, I'll send him to sparrow heaven lickety-split!"
But JT loved the sparrow's chirping and the bird never

stayed away from its cage for long. One time Jasper had *dropped* a little present on JT's shirt while perched on his shoulder. JT quickly cleaned up the wet mess, leaving no tell-tale remains for Mommy to discover. He had breathed a sigh of relief that Jasper had done his business on him, and not on the Berber. He strictly warned Jasper that if he wanted to stay alive he would need to be more careful.

When Daddy and Mommy asked Grandma what in the world she wanted with a pet sparrow, she had an immediate response: "In the springtime folks get all excited when they spot a robin. No one ever gets excited over sparrows. They're just such common, ordinary little birds. But God says He notices when even one sparrow falls to the ground. Then He tells us that we are worth more to Him than many sparrows. Jasper is a good reminder that even someone as plain and ordinary as me is important to God and that He will always watch over me!"

That was that... Daddy and Mommy almost always gave in to Grandma. She had a way of quoting Bible verses that would shut everyone up real quick. JT wished Grandma was still here. Maybe she would know a Bible verse that would help him figure out what was going on with his father and mother.

"Maybe they're jist fergettin' 'bout Christmas," JT reasoned. "Maybe I jist need to remind 'em." So he hopped from his bed, determined to tackle the problem head on.

He found both his parents sitting at the kitchen table. It was unusual for his father to be home from work so early. He typically put in long days building new homes. It seemed like he'd been around the house a lot more lately. His parents had been talking quietly but stopped as soon as he entered the room.

"Daddy, when are wc goin' t'git our Christmas tree?" he began. "Ya know Christmas is comin' fast."

His father looked at his mother and then sighed. "I know that, Son," his Dad responded. "But I'm afraid we'll have no tree this year. Econ'my is real bad, JT. Real bad! Just won't allow for us to buy a Christmas tree. Some folks are saying depression could be coming too, and then I won't have any work at all. Sorry, JT."

"Don't worry, Son," his mother continued with what seemed like only a half-hearted smile. "We'll still have some presents and a nice dinner on Christmas day. But this bad economy's forcing everyone to cut back."

His parents looked almost as sad as they had when Grandma died. JT always thought his dad could fix anything, so why couldn't he fix this? But he knew better than to argue when his father lookcd so serious. JT ran back to his bedroom and flopped on his bed.

"No Christmas tree!" he cried aloud to Jasper. He thought about how his family always drove to the tree farm to pick just the perfect tree. He thought about the twinkling lights and shiny red balls that made it look so beautiful. He thought about how lonely the presents would look with no wonderful-smelling pine boughs hanging over them.

Jasper chirped as if trying to cheer up his young friend. JT opened the cage so Jasper could fly around. As the little brown bird circled the room, JT watched him sorrowfully. "I wish I could fly around like you Jasper. If I could, I'd go find that mean ol' E. Conmy. I don't know who he is," he declared, "but I'd find him somehow and then I'd punch Mr. Conmy right in the nose! And I'd git you to peck him on the head!"

Jasper landed on his bed and hopped from square to square of the old quilt hand-made by his grandmother. He thought about Grandma. He knew she wouldn't have wanted him to punch anybody in the nose. Grandma was big on forgiveness. She always said that, if Jesus was willing to forgive her for all her sins, how could she refuse to forgive people who sinned against her? Then she would quote some Bible verse about asking God to forgive us, like we forgive our enemies. No doubt about it, Grandma would have suggested something other than beating up E. Conmy. But what? JT watched his grandmother's little bird pecking at a quilt patch and suddenly an idea popped into his head.

"Why... I'll jist make a Christmas tree!" he decided. "Daddy jist said that guy won't allow us to *buy* one. He didn't say we can't *make* one!" JT lay back on the pillow and put his hands behind his head. He had some serious planning to do!

Over the next 10 days, JT focused on little else. He wanted to carry out his project in secret, and surprise Daddy and Mommy on Christmas morning. Since his father had already taught JT lots about wood and tools, he was sure he could create a simple tree all by himself. But he would need to take advantage of every opportunity that presented itself, to steal time alone in Daddy's workshop.

On the first day of the week, with Jasper perched in his favorite spot on JT's flannel-clad shoulder, the child set to work. He hunted through a pile of scrap wood and discovered two long pine studs. They would be perfect! He would use one for the trunk. It was about twice as

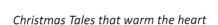

tall as he was and would make a good-sized tree. He would cut the other into pieces for the branches.

Days two and three were spent sawing and painting. It wasn't the easiest task for a seven-year-old, but back and forth he pushed and pulled on that saw. Jasper sat on the tool bench and cheered him on with his chirping. Finally JT succeeded in cutting the second piece of lumber into three different-sized sections... a short, medium and long... for branches. The end of each board was kind of rough, with a few splinters that poked out dangerously but he figured that would just make his tree more realistic. He found a half-full can of brown paint on a top shelf and, although he had never attempted a paint job before, he managed to get a rather sloppy coat on all the pieces. JT was ecstatic!

The fourth day he searched for long nails and a hammer with which to attach the branches. Daddy had drawers and drawers full of nails and screws of all different sizes. And his tools were scattered all over the shelves. JT could understand why Mommy was always fussing at Daddy to clean up his shop. It sure would have made things easier if everything would have been in plain sight. He finally found what he needed and attached each branch with a long carpenter's nail through the center and into the "trunk." He leaned his creation against the wall and stood back to survey his work.

"Well... the *shape* is right," JT critiqued, "but it really needs dec'rations t'make it perfect. Yeah... then it'll be beautiful!" Satisfied, he hid his tree behind the old ping-pong table that leaned against the wall of the shop. Tomorrow, day five, he would look for ornaments.

This proved even more difficult than finding the hammer and nails. "Wow, Mommy says Daddy should clean up his shop, but the attic's even worse! And most of this junk is Mommy's stuff." Jasper seemed to like the attic. He flew from rafter to rafter and chirped his encouragement to JT. The boy wasn't sure where to start looking for the boxes of Christmas tree decorations. Finally after poking around in dozens of boxes and sneezing at least fifty times from the dust bunnies flying through the air, he found just what he was looking for... a box with red shiny ornaments, a strand of gold tinsel and a long string of Christmas lights. When the coast was clear, he sneaked them down to his bedroom.

On the sixth day, JT wanted to add the lights to his tree. He soon discovered this was no simple job. He just couldn't figure a way to attach the lights to the boards. After several attempts, he sat on the shop floor and rested his chin on his hands in exasperation. He felt like giving up. He didn't know what to do! Just then Jasper chirped and it seemed as if JT heard Grandma preaching one of her sermons, "Perseverance, JT! Difficulties help us learn to persevere. Perseverance is not

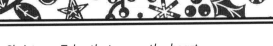

giving up when the going gets tough. Remember, it is always darkest right before the dawn. When things are especially hard, thank God that He is going to help you. And He will!"

JT had heard Grandma preach this over and over, along with dozens of other life lessons. "Okay God. I'm not gonna give up. But I'm gonna ask You t' help me 'cuz I don't have a clue what t' do." Then remembering Grandma's advice, he added, "Oh yeah, and thank You fer helpin' me pers'vere!"

He looked over at Jasper who was pecking at what looked like a brown worm on Daddy's work bench. He went to investigate (as boys are bound to do when worms are suspected). It turned out to be just a rubber band. "Jasper, don't eat that! It could make ya sick!" He snatched the band from the bird.

"That's it!" He grabbed the lights once more, along with a handful of rubber bands from Daddy's shelf and started attaching the strand to the boards, beginning at the top and zig-zagging downward. When he reached the bottom of the tree, he simply wrapped the remaining string around the trunk, finishing up with just enough cord to reach a wall outlet. "Wow! Grandma was right!" he thought. "Thanks, God!"

Day seven was much easier. He had helped Mommy bend paper clips last year to make hooks. In short order he had 12 shiny red, tear-drop-shaped ornaments hanging on paper clips, hooked through rubber bands on each branch.

Days eight and nine, JT gathered small twigs from the blue spruce tree in his backyard. Then with great globs of Elmer's, he glued them strategically to the branches and trunk of his tree.

On day 10, JT took Jasper to admire the finished product. He didn't have a star, so around the top he looped the short piece of gold tinsel he'd found with the other ornaments. There! It was finished! Jasper chirped and JT would have too if it wouldn't have brought his mother snooping. He couldn't wait to sneak his masterpiece into the house on Christmas Eve and lean it against the living room wall right where their usual tree stood. Daddy and Mommy would be so happy. He was sure of it!

All would have been set for a super Christmas had Jasper the house sparrow not vanished the very next day! JT discovered the door of Jasper's cage open as well as the door to the garage. The bird's young owner was heart-broken. He knew his little friend wouldn't last long

in cold wintry weather. He was used to being pampered. He wouldn't have any idea how to survive on his own.

Mommy said Jasper was a survivor and there was a good chance he would come back. But JT knew she was concerned. She kept going to the kitchen window and looking out. Daddy said, "These things happen, Son," and shook his head sadly. JT wondered if E. Conmy or D. Preshun were somehow responsible for Jasper's disappearance. Christmas would be miserable without his best pal!

Two more days passed and Jasper had not returned! JT was sick with fear and sadness.

December 24 arrived and JT moped around the house all day. He was so lonely for Jasper he almost forgot all about his Christmas tree surprise.

But when his parents finally headed up to bed, JT remembered and sneaked out to the garage. He uncovered the tree, hidden behind the ping-pong table. Mustering every bit of strength he possessed, he hoisted it over his shoulder. Then, trying desperately to keep it from crashing to the floor, he lugged it slowly into the living room. Breathing hard from the weight and the thrill of secrecy, JT propped the tree against the wall, right in back of the nativity set that had belonged to Grandma. He inserted the dangling plug into the outlet and stood back to survey his creation. Without

Jasper, the tree didn't look nearly so beautiful. In fact, he thought it looked pretty silly and ugly. Nothing was turning out right.

He missed Jasper. He missed Grandma. He missed his parents being happy. He missed the usual big bushy pine tree. What an un-merry Christmas!

He laid down on the floor, put his head on his arms and cried.

Then gently, like a far-away thought, he heard his Grandma's no-nonsense voice. "Remember JT, faith is believing what you *don't* see! If you can see something, that's nice, but then you don't need any faith. Faith is believing your prayer is answered even before you see an answer. Without faith, it is impossible to please God... so the tough times give us the best opportunity to make the Lord happy. Always trust God to do even more than what you could imagine possible!"

"Okay, God," JT muttered. "I don't know how Yer gonna do it. And Yer gonna haf t'work fast. But I'm gonna b'lieve jist like Grandma would've, that You kin somehow make this Christmas turn out all right... in fact, even better than all right!"

He stood to his feet, took a paper from the desk in the corner and in simple, second-grade printing, left a note under the tree for his parents to find in the morning. Then he tiptoed back to his bedroom, stopping just long enough to open the front door of the house just a little.

Right before sunrise Christmas morning, two bathrobed parents stopped in amazement when they entered the living room. JT's tree leaned precariously against the wall. The glued-on twigs had already lost most of their needles. The jagged two-by-four branches, attached by three half-hammered nails, tilted in varying angles. The rubber-banded lights crisscrossed from one side to the other, the paper-clipped red balls hung like drops of blood, and the straggly tinsel crowned the top.

His father picked up JT's hastily-scrawled note.

"Dear Daddy and Mommy. I mayd this tree. I hope it mayks ya smile. I only used two boards and three nails. I hope E. Conmee and D. Preshun won't mind. Merrey Christmas! P. S. I love ya lotz!"

They gazed again at the crudely-made tree by the manger. There, portrayed right in front of them, was the Christmas story… the infant Jesus, overshadowed by a son's sacrificial gift! JT's hand-made creation reflected so beautifully God's timeless message of love! Daddy

grinned and cleared the lump from his throat. Mommy wiped tears from her eyes.

And when Jerome T. Jones, clad in his faded flannel pajamas, burst into the room minutes later, he found his parents, arms around each other, still standing in front of his tree, holding his note and smiling the biggest smiles he'd seen in a very long time.

"Merry Christmas, JT," his parents greeted him joyfully. His mother hugged him tight. His father laughed and roughed up his son's already messy hair. Then giggling likc scven-year-olds themselves, they turned back toward the tree and pointed to the few presents beneath. "Come on… let's open our gifts!" JT dropped to his knees and reached eagerly for the first colorfully-wrapped box.

Suddenly a tiny brown-feathered head popped up from between the packages. It eyed the family for just a moment and then launched into a sparrow song sweeter than any Christmas carol!

"Jasper!" JT erupted with delight. The little sparrow promptly flew to his young friend's shoulder, chirping more merrily than ever. JT reached up and began to lovingly stroke the little bird's black-banded neck.

"I kin hardly b'lieve yer here, Jasper!" he sighed.

Another merry chirp sounded, but this time it didn't come from Jasper's beak.

JT and his parents turned back toward the manger. Peeking above the side of baby Jesus' bed, was another brown-feathered head, slightly paler than Jasper's. With a sudden flutter of wings it circled around their heads and came to perch on the very top of JT's tree.

"Look! Jasper brought a friend home with him!" JT exclaimed.

"I'd say, he brought a *girl* friend home," his dad laughed. "Or maybe *Mrs.* Jasper."

"I can't believe it! Two birds! I have two birds now! I'm gonna call her... Jasmine!" JT announced. "I *can* keep her, can't I, Daddy and Mommy?" he pleaded.

His father scratched his head. "Well, E. Conmee and D. Preshun may have affected the amount of money in this household, but apparently they've had no effect on the sparrow population." He looked toward his wife, who threw up her arms in despair. But then grinning, she nodded, "Yes, you may keep her!"

JT jumped to his feet and pranced in circles around the living room. Jasper did a couple of laps himself, finally alighting next to Jasmine on the top of their young master's tree.

"Wow!" JT paused in his victory dance and looked up at the birds. "God made this a super Christmas after all! Just like I asked Him to!"

His parents shook their heads in amazement. Then suddenly his father's expression changed and he eyed JT suspiciously. "I wonder just how Jasper and his girl managed to get into the house." JT looked guiltily toward the front hall. His father's gaze followed. "Hmmm," he tilted his head in the direction of the front door. "Who in the world left that door open all night? Do you have any idea, JT?" His voice was stern, but his eyes twinkled.

JT raised his eyebrows and shrugged his shoulders. He glanced toward his new sparrow friends singing joyously from the tree-top. "Don't blame me, Dad!" he exclaimed as he ran to close the door. "I think ya oughta blame Grandma!"

Sing to the Lord a new song;
sing to the Lord,
all the earth.

Sing to the Lord,
praise his name;
proclaim his salvation
day after day.

Psalm 96:1-2

Charlie's Song

Charlie's my 12-year-old kid brother. He's also our household's bathroom boom box! You know what I mean don't you? He's the family member that serenades from the shower, bellows out melodies in the bathtub, and croons from the commode. When he enters the bathroom, I might as well forget about getting in for another hour or so, because Charlie has just disappeared into his musical kingdom. He sure knows how to pest a 14-year-old sister. After all, being a cool adolescent in the 90's requires all the mirror minutes possible, and the best reflection I get is at the bathroom vanity. It wouldn't be so bad if we had two bathrooms but, since our house is cursed with only one, Charlie's lengthy solos are not appreciated! At least they *weren't...* until suddenly last December when the music stopped.

Charlie has always liked to sing. I remember when he was a baby he would bounce in his car seat to the rhythms on the radio and "goo-ga" along with the tunes. Sometimes I'd stuff a mitten in his mouth to shut him up, but Dad or Mom always made me take it out. They said I shouldn't stifle Charlie's God-given talent. *Talent, schmalent!* It was noise to me. As he got older, at least the melodies became somewhat recognizable, but they

still bugged me! If he wasn't sure of the lyrics, that didn't matter. He'd squeeze in any old words he would dream up whether they fit or not. He'd sing at the supper table and his choice of dining music was disgusting. I'll never forget the time I was just ready to bite into a delicious-smelling baked pork chop when Charlie belted out, "Old McDonald had a pig. E-I-E-I-O. With an oink, please don't eat me, and an oink, please don't eat me..."

That did it! I wadded up two paper napkins, stuck them in my ears and glared at the little pest. God-given or not, there was no reason why I should have to starve because of my kid brother's vocal genius.

Over the years, his musical taste grew along with his size. From Sunday school songs and nursery rhyme tunes he graduated to more mature stuff like hymns, choruses, and themes from Broadway musicals. I remember when he sang "If I were a rich man, daidle, deedle, daidle digguh, digguh, deedle, daidle, dum," over and over until I felt like gagging. I began to make up my own lyrics to keep from screaming. So when he'd start singing, I'd mentally substitute my own words, "If I were a rich man, I would pay a guy to put a garbage can on Charlie's head!" Dad and Mom would not have been pleased had they known my thoughts. And when the evangelist visited our church, I repented to God for such nasty desires but, during Charlie's Fiddler on the Roof craze, I wasn't that pious and so my vengeful thoughts ran unchecked.

His singing became an inescapable cross for me to bear. By December of last year, it had reached the pinnacle of irritation. If only he wouldn't sing *in the bathroom!* Not only did he rob me of precious grooming time, but that's where he always used what I call his opera volume. He'd start singing softly, but then I'd hear the crescendo beginning. Before long his changing adolescent voice would be screeching out a warbly falsetto that was so loud it drowned out the sounds of the running water, the dog barking, the traffic on the highway in front of our house, and the sitcom I was watching on TV! Was there nowhere to find peace from this pest? Maybe the angel of the Lord had proclaimed peace on earth, but I figured he hadn't reckoned with Charlie in our bathroom.

Usually in December... no, I take that back... in late November, Charlie began his Christmas repertoire. Typically he latched onto one or two Christmas carols and milked them dry. I mean he sang them so often, even he got sick of them. Last year started out to be no exception. Charlie "rocked around the Christmas tree" every morning in the shower. And he "glo-o-or-i-ahed" with the angels he had heard on high, every evening in the bathtub. I never could figure out why Dad and Mom

allowed such senseless waste of precious hot water. My brother had to be the cleanest kid in junior high!

And then, one morning in early December, the second floor of our house was strangely silent. Charlie wasn't singing! Actually, it didn't dawn on me that Charlie had kept quiet until we were on our way out the door to get the school bus and he didn't try to trip me, like he usually did. Then it hit me... no music... no pestiness. There had to be something wrong with Charlie.

I thought it was great! Peace and quiet at last. I reveled in it. For the first time in my life I could loiter in the bathroom, because Charlie wasn't there singing. I basked in the delightful new feeling. Silence. Sweet stillness! For the first week, it felt indescribable. For part of the second week it felt good. But by the end of that week, it felt weird! I began to get worried... worried about Charlie. What had robbed my brother of his song?

For the next week and a half, I became an amateur detective. I watched Charlie every possible moment. He seemed strange and kind of sad. I sneaked into his bedroom and searched for any clue... maybe a love note from a girl at school. No, Charlie wasn't interested in girls yet, except those he could pest. I even hid just around the corner in the hallway, listening for any sound that might come from the bathroom. Impossible though it seemed, I actually was hoping he might start singing again, but... nothing!

Finally, I was desperate and I did what most kids leave 'til their last resort. I went to my parents. "Dad, Mom, I need to talk to you about something." That always gets parents panicking! They tend to imagine the worst, like you're going to tell them you're flunking algebra or that you've been considering running away from home. Dad put down his paper immediately and Mom dropped her mug in the kitchen sink and quickly plunked down on the sofa by Dad. I had their full attention. "It's about Charlie... he's not singing. I mean I should be glad for that, but it just seems like something's wrong with him. Is he sick or something?" I stopped, feeling dangerously close to crying.

When I glanced at them, was that a tear in Mom's eye too? Dad pulled me down beside him and put his arm around me. "I think Charlie's just really missing Grandpa, Honey. This will be the first Christmas without him. We all miss him terribly, but you know Grandpa and Charlie were real buddies. I think it has just dawned on Charlie how strange the holidays will seem without him."

Could that really be it? How did parents figure things out like that? Seemed too simple, and yet it was true that Christmas wouldn't be the same this year.

Grandpa had added a special sparkle to the whole season. He was the one who fell right smack into the middle of the Christmas tree one year when he was trying to put the star on top. Grandma had been upset about the ruined tree until he reminded her that he was the one with pine needles sticking into his behind and lights blinking all around his head. Then we had all started laughing and laughed until we cried. What a memory! He was the one who put paper grocery bags over our heads on Christmas morning and led us through the family room, so we wouldn't get even a glimpse of our gifts until after breakfast. It was Grandpa who always read with a catch in his voice, the story of Jesus' birth on Christmas morning. It was Grandpa who wore that crazy Santa Claus hat while he cooked the turkey. It was Grandpa who loaded everybody in his van and drove us around to see the lights, all the time singing Christmas carols. He was off-key and didn't know most of the words, but with Grandpa we didn't mind. It was Grandpa who always prayed God's blessing over the whole family for the new year.

But this year he was gone. Could that really be what was bothering Charlie? And if it was, what could be done to cheer him up? After all, no one could bring Grandpa back.

I began to actually pray for Charlie. I asked God to do something, anything to bring my brother back to normal. And I asked Him to hurry. I mean, Christmas without Grandpa would be tough enough, but it was almost like I'd lost my brother too. I wanted the old singing Charlie home for the holidays!

Christmas week arrived. Still no sounds from the bathroom. Still no pestering from Charlie. I was beginning to give up hope. I was scared to even mention Grandpa to Charlie, for fear of making the whole situation even worse.

Christmas Eve came and, like good Christian kids, Charlie and I hustled off to church with our parents to take part in the annual candlelight service. This year the youth and adult choirs were combining to be the angelic host. The little kids were going to have the bathrobe parts. We gathered in the church basement along with the other choir members and put on our white sheet costumes draped with gold tinsel. I thought everybody looked pretty funny, especially Charlie with his enormous orange and black sneakers and faded blue jeans sticking out from below the sheet. I teased him about his dangling shoelaces but Charlie just shrugged. Some joyous angel he was going to be this year. I wondered if he'd even open his mouth.

Finally the time came for us to head toward the sanctuary for our glorious appearance. Charlie and I were right at the end of the line. Just ahead of us

was one of the senior choir members... a white-haired, funny-looking man that I had never met personally. He seemed to know us and our family 'cause he'd talked to us real friendly-like while we were putting on our robes, but I didn't even know his name. We followed him and the rest of the group up the back staircase, through the prayer room, down the hallway, up two more steps and finally into the candlelit auditorium. It was a beautiful atmosphere. I even forgot Charlie temporarily and let myself really enjoy the moment. We repeated our, "Glory to God in the highest, and on earth peace, good-will toward men," and then sang our "glorias." At least *I* sang. I didn't hear any sounds coming from Charlie at all.

It seemed to be over much too quickly. Then our angel procession was heading toward the middle steps of the platform to exit down the center aisle. The room was still. A reverent hush was over the congregation. A lone violin played "Silent Night" so sweetly and peacefully. The congregation held their little white candles in their little white cups and the sight of the auditorium full of flickering lights was mesmerizing. I was carried away by the heavenly feel of it all.

And then it happened! Those dangling shoelaces of Charlie's dragged behind him and wouldn't you know? I stepped right smack on the longest one. Before I knew what was happening, Charlie lurched forward, almost knocking over that nice old man in front of him. Trying desperately to regain his balance, my brother lunged backward and grabbed me. My feet flew out from under me and I flung my angel wings and beat the air, but it was no use! Charlie and I tumbled thunderously down the steps, landing in an unangelic heap of white sheets, gold tinsel and tilted halos right at the front of the church! Somehow Charlie's arms had hooked my tinsel and we were hopelessly intertwined. He'd even managed to lose a shoe in the process and now his giant Converse sat alone on the next-to-top step.

It would have been hilarious, had it not been so embarrassing! To make matters worse, the whole angel procession had gone on ahead. Charlie and I were center stage, alone and feeling very foolish. I closed my eyes and wished for five long seconds that this was only a dream. When I opened my eyes and looked up, there was the old gentleman angel who had been ahead of Charlie, leaning over us. He was gently pulling tinsel free and he had retrieved Charlie's sneaker. "Don't you worry, kids," he whispered with a twinkle in his eye, "this old angel's gonna wait for you!" And then he started to chuckle... a soft, infectious chuckle just like the way Grandpa used to chuckle. I looked at Charlie and we both grinned. He pulled on his shoe.

I guess the whole church full of people had been so stunned by everything that they just sat there like statues at first, but then someone began to laugh and, before you know it, the whole place was roaring in laughter. Most of the candles went out just from being laughed on. It was undoubtedly the only Nativity the church members had ever seen that included two *fallen* angels.

Charlie and I picked ourselves up, hooked arms with our rescuer and accompanied the old man down the aisle while everyone, including Mary and Joseph and the shepherds, continued to laugh and applaud. What a memorable Christmas Eve this had turned out to be!

Later, on the way home in the car, Charlie and I were quiet for awhile in the back seat. Then he leaned over to me and said, "Hey, Sis, what did that old man say to us when he came back to help us tonight?"

I had to think a minute. "Umm... I think he said, 'this old angel's gonna wait for you,' or something like that."

"Yeah," Charlie said thoughtfully, "that's what I thought he said too."

And then I took a risk. "His laugh sure sounded like Grandpa's didn't it?" Charlie nodded.

I took a chance and pushed on..."And, I guess that's exactly what Grandpa's doing for us too... waiting for us. Don't ya think?"

Charlie just sat silent for a minute. Maybe I shouldn't have dared to mention Grandpa. Then my kid brother grinned. And it was almost an old Charlie grin. "Yeah, I guess he is!"

That night before heading upstairs to get ready for bed, I stopped by the nativity set in the living room and just stared at the scene. God really loved us so much! I silently thanked the Lord for coming to earth to die so that we could have eternal life. I thanked Him too for the comfort of knowing Grandpa would be waiting for us in heaven. I prayed again that Charlie would know that same comfort. Then I climbed the steps to the second floor. Arriving at the top, I paused just around the corner from the bathroom.

Was that what I thought it was or was it just my imagination? No, it was the real thing! *Charlie was singing!* But what was he singing? It sounded like the tune to "Angels We Have Heard on High," but the lyrics were different. I stuck my ear against the door and listened. The "gloria" part was the same, but what was that last line? It wasn't "in excelsis Deo." It sounded like he'd crammed a bunch of words... in typical Charlie fashion... into those last two measures. Charlie's voice

grew louder. The old opera bellow was back and the words came through loud and clear, "Glo-o-o-oria, Jesus and Grandpa are waiting for me! Glo-o-o-o-ria, Jesus and Grandpa are waiting for me!"

I leaned against the bathroom door, sighed, smiled, and wiped the happy tears from my eyes. I knew Charlie's voice would probably be "rockin around the Christmas tree" any moment. And I figured I wouldn't get in the bathroom for a very, very long time. But I didn't care. If Grandpa and Jesus could wait for Charlie, I guessed I could too!

Author's Note:
This story is dedicated to...

four musical children and a musical husband
who have filled our home
with melody, harmony and rhythm
in and out of the bathroom...

and to two wonderful Grandpas
who are missed very much by our family,
but who are both waiting in heaven,
along with Jesus, for the rest of us!

After The Curtain Fell

Having Jessica for a sister had its moments.
Some good, some bad… but most of the time…
memorable! In fact, one of Jessica's Christmas
moments turned my life around for good!

When I was just a little guy, Jessica made a wonderful playmate. Being only a year apart, we spent hours in innocent, childish pursuits. We had great times playing horsey, house, and hide and seek. She was the older sibling which, in most cases, would have made her the boss but, for some reason, she always preferred following me around, attempting to copy every move I made. Folks never referred to us as "Jessica and Jeremy." It was always "Jeremy and Jessica" which I thought strange since she was the firstborn.

It wasn't until I reached the ripe age of six that I realized why Jessica would never assume leadership over me. Jessica was different. My parents sat me down one evening and explained that their only daughter was born with a problem in her brain. That first talk didn't give me much detail but, through the years that followed, I came to understand more fully what her disorder meant for Jessica, for me, and for our family.

My father was the pastor of a fairly large church, which meant people were always asking us about our "dear little girl." We wanted to be as positive as possible so we went through the whole gamut of politically-correct terms for Jessica... handicapped, disabled, physically and mentally challenged, special-needs child... just when I would get used to using one label, a new one would come into vogue.

But changing the term didn't change Jessica. She was always the same... a perpetual five-year-old. She wore a brace on her leg, which caused her to limp. That didn't stop her from getting wherever she wanted to go. I could always hear her approaching... her thump-drag gait was unmistakable. And it usually followed *me* wherever I went! I was obviously Jessica's favorite person. And I came to believe that my name was also Jessica's favorite word, because she would repeat it over and over as a preface to anything she asked me. "Jeremy, Jeremy, Jeremy, play with me?" "Jeremy, Jeremy, Jeremy, read me story!" Her pronunciation wasn't too good so "Jeremy" usually sounded like "Germy." Some of my buddies overheard her calling me this and, much to my embarrassment, latched onto it as a nickname. I didn't particularly appreciate being referred to as bacteria!

One of Jessica's unique traits was her total lack of pretense. She was who she was. What she felt she expressed, which wasn't always at socially-acceptable

moments. I'll never forget the worship service when Jessica had an "attack" of flatulence just as my father uttered the solemn words, "Let us all bow for prayer." The explosive noise was so loud the whole congregation heard it, including my dad. He had to pause a moment to get control (I opened one eye and saw his mouth twitching as he tried desperately to stifle a chuckle). Then, just as he pulled himself together and began, "Our dear heavenly Father," Jessica's high-pitched voice rang out, "Oh, *ex-sc-oo-oo-se* me!" Well, that sent the whole place into convulsions of laughter. Dad gave up on the prayer and ended with an abrupt "Amen."

Then there was the time that Jessica decided to show off some newly-acquired knowledge. My mother had shared with Jessica and me that God was going to give our family another baby. I already knew the basic "birds and bees" stuff, but Jessica had never had "the talk." So my mom explained to my sister that the baby was growing inside her tummy, and that ladies' stomachs get bigger when this is happening. That week at Prayer Meeting we sat beside Mrs. Worthington... the wealthiest and most distinguished lady in our congregation. She was a rather large woman, always prim, proper, poised and perfectly dressed. Imagine my mother's humiliation when Jessica piped up at prayer request time, "Pray for Mrs. Worthington (only it came out like 'Wart-in-town'). She has baby in her fat belly. Mommy told me!" I never saw two women turn such a

brilliant shade of red at the same time. It's a wonder Mrs. Worthington kept attending our church!

And there were Jessica's shrieks. At any moment she would let loose with one of her unique squeals of happiness. Those shrieks were ear-piercing and, when I was a kid, they caused me to immediately clap my hands over my ears. Their timing was completely unpredictable! In fact, I don't think that Jessica herself knew when one was coming. They began as a contented "Ah, Ah, Ah," but then a shrill, prolonged screech would erupt, followed by a satisfied chuckle that just sort of faded away softly. For Jessica, these were expressions of pure, unbridled delight! And those shrieks were frequent because Jessica was delighted most of the time. It was nice that Jessica found life so joyful. However, for those of us close to her, these outbursts were unnerving to say the least!

All in all, Jessica's abnormality came to seem pretty normal to me and, most of the time, I was very glad to be her little brother. Our relationship changed, of course, as the years progressed. For a brief period in junior high, I tried to hide the fact that she was my sister. This stemmed from a smart-allecky seventh grader's question, "Hey, Jeremy... is that stupid girl your sister?" But hiding Jessica was impossible. If she was anywhere in my vicinity, I could count on my name being broadcast. "Jermy, Jermy, Jermy!" Anonymity

was a lost cause. By the time high school rolled around, I had once again accepted my lot in life as Jessica's brother and had become instead her protector. In fact, I discovered that looking out for such a sister actually boosted my image in the eyes of some tenderhearted females I was hoping to impress!

When the day finally came for me to leave for college, I had to duck out of the house when Jessica wasn't looking. I hated departing that way and I had to blink back a couple of tears. But, after Dad and Mom explained to Jessica that I would be leaving, she had attached herself to my body from morning 'til night. Though still a child in mind, she now had a five-foot, 115-pound adult body. So, I figured it would be easier to escape while she was sleeping rather than try to wrench myself from her desperate clutch.

Being away from home, and Jessica, seemed strange at first. I was so used to her incessant jabber, her comical swaying walk, and her ear-piercing shrieks. We had always seemed connected. But I soon settled into exciting college life, thinking less and less of Jessica and home. Dorm life replaced Jessica with "never a dull moment." Professors surpassed my parents with their apparent wisdom and insight. I began questioning things I had never doubted. I began toying with temptations I had always avoided. I felt like a veil had descended between me and my old environment, my old beliefs, my old life. My deeply-engrained Christian theology seemed distant and unfamiliar.

The first semester flew by quickly and, in what seemed an amazingly short amount of time, I was home for the holidays. Except, I didn't really feel "at home." I felt more like a stranger, an outsider. Even Jessica, who had always made me smile, seemed pitiful to me. Her abnormality was more glaring than ever. "If God is the loving God He's supposed to be," I questioned for the first time, "then why does He make people like Jessica? And if Jesus healed those who came to Him, why doesn't He heal Jessica's mind? Is Jesus even God? Is there even a God?"

Jessica seemed oblivious to the barrier that blocked me from her. She shrieked and chortled like always and relegated me to my "germ" status on a regular basis. Like most families, we bustled through pre-holiday activities... gift buying, tree-decorating, baking, cleaning, and on and on. And of course, since my dad was a pastor, there was the inevitable Christmas Eve pageant with all its preparations. I had agreed to help him with set and props, even though my heart was not in the subject matter. It all seemed rather trite to me.

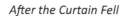

I picked up a cheap baby doll at the local discount store, to replace the church's old "baby Jesus," who had lost an arm and a leg over the years. When Jessica spied the doll, she let out a shriek and begged to hold it. "Jermy, Jermy, Jermy, ple-ee-ee-se me hold baby?!" Her question/command irritated me and I gave her a firm, "No, this baby is not for you, Jessica!" I turned and walked away, before she could nag any further.

For the next several days, every time Jessica saw me she asked for the baby and every time I brushed her off with, "NO, Jessica... that baby is not for you!" I didn't like myself for the way I was treating her, but I rationalized that I wasn't the same person anymore... my world was expanding... both Jessica and Jesus no longer fit!

The Christmas Eve pageant went the way of all pageants. Kids in kimonos with towels on their heads did their shepherd thing. Toddlers with tinsel halos fumbled their way through "Gloria, in Excelsis Deo." I sat in the back pew watching the whole event like a visitor from another place in time. I was a spectator, not a participant. I looked at the congregation. "How can they buy into all this fantasy?" I wondered. "I really don't need this anymore. I think it's time for me to let Jesus go." My thoughts ran further and further away.

Two bed sheets on a crude frame served to separate one scene from the next and two junior high boys had

been recruited to man the curtain. As the play ended, they drew the sheets one final time and I felt like it symbolized the termination of my childish beliefs and values.

People began to mingle and chat with one another. I sat thinking how wise I was becoming, and yet wondering why I felt more alone and empty than I had ever felt in my life.

Probably no one will ever know how it happened. Perhaps a renegade toddler angel caught a wired wing in the fabric. Perhaps a sly pre-teen thought it would be a cool prank to give the drapes a little pull. At any rate, no one will forget the crash of that frame and curtain toppling off the stage and onto the communion table below. Startled, everyone pivoted toward the platform... this time to assess damage rather than drama.

And there, on the other side of the fallen curtain, was... my sister. Had Jessica caused the disaster? Maybe, maybe not. But there she was, kneeling center-stage by the orange-crate manger. With a gleeful lunge, she grabbed the baby Jesus doll and lifted him high. I'll never know how she knew where I was seated, but she suddenly pointed right at me and shouted, "Jermy, Jermy, Jermy, I found Jesus! He is for me!" She squeezed the baby tightly and then looked back at me. "Jermy, Jermy, Jermy, He is for you, too!" Then with an intonation that was half question, half command,

she shrieked, "Keep Him?! Jermy, Jermy, keep Him?!" Was she asking permission or was she giving me an impassioned command as someone who seemed to know much more than I?

In that Jessica moment, I heard the quiet voice of God invading my thoughts. "She knows the truth about me, Jeremy. Do *you* dare to hold onto the truth? Will *you* keep Me, Jeremy?"

I looked back at Jessica who had plopped back down on the platform, cradling the baby doll. But she wasn't looking at the baby... her innocent, yet penetrating, gaze was fixed on me.

"Yes, Jessica." I mouthed the words. I pointed to her and then turned my finger toward my heart. "We will both keep Him!" And I knew that something was settled for me in that moment that nothing would ever undo.

Jessica looked at me and smiled. I smiled back. The veil between us was gone. Then she turned her attention back to the baby. And, I could feel it coming. It started with the, "Ah, Ah, Ah" and then, from deep inside her, erupted the most jubilant shriek I'd ever heard! Outwardly, I chuckled, but my heart was SHOUTING with her!

I wondered if God had actually designed Jessica to be *my* protector? "Perhaps," I thought, "one day, when we get to heaven, we'll discover that the Jessicas of this

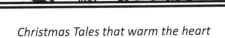
life are, after all, the truly normal ones and the rest of us are sorely lacking. And when that curtain falls," I concluded, "I will shriek with joy to witness Jessica's greatest moment!"

The Christmas Sack

S am hoisted the heavy pack onto his back, tugged on thick work gloves and pulled a red wool cap over his unruly blond hair. With a quick hug for Carly, his 15-year-old kid sister, and a warning to not be late for school, he hurried out the door of their tiny apartment. He would have to hurry himself, so as to not miss the bus to the city center. He had long ago decided to never be late for work.

As he jogged along the sidewalk, Sam adjusted his home-made backpack... an old but sturdy white canvas feed sack he had found along the fence at a former job site. He had attached a bungee cord to the top to tie it closed and seat belts rescued from a child's discarded car seat to serve as shoulder straps. With denim salvaged from a pair of Carly's outgrown jeans, he hand-sewed a couple of patch pockets inside to conceal his wallet and important papers. The main compartment of the bag transported a hodge-podge of carpentry tools, a peanut butter sandwich for lunch and a flannel shirt in case he needed an extra layer in cold weather. On the outside of the sack Carly, to surprise him on his birthday, had glued flashy pink sequins... S-A-M. He was more than a little embarrassed by this addition, but

knew she had been so excited to add her touch. So he thanked her and put up with plenty of amused stares.

He made it to the bus stop just in time and, breathing hard, climbed aboard. It seemed to the broad-shouldered 25-year-old that he was always in a rush. Somewhere way back in his brain were memories of a slower-paced time, but he rarely let his thoughts travel there. This morning however, as he settled into a seat and gazed out the bus window, he allowed himself to reminisce. After all, it was December 1. Christmas decorations were everywhere, and the holidays always made him nostalgic... and kind of sad too. His thoughts immediately went to his family.

Sam had one mental image of his father... smiling and swinging his little boy onto his strong shoulders. Sam remembered how he held onto his father's ears and laughed as his dad galloped around their little yard, his son bouncing and giggling on his high perch. But an accident claimed his father's life when Sam was just three and, as hard as he tried, Sam couldn't remember anything else about the man. He knew he had existed. But now he was no more than a smiling face in a photograph.

On the other hand, memories of his mother were vivid. The tragic loss of her young husband quickly took its toll on her. She worked hard but money was always tight. She and Sam moved often, always to a smaller

and dingier place. Then there was the unexpected arrival of Carly when he was ten. His mom explained to Sam that she had hoped to find a new father for him, but the boyfriend she invited into their home for a few months took off as soon as the baby arrived. Sam loved his little sister and was fiercely protective of her. But another person to feed and clothe meant even more financial pressure. Sam's jaw tightened as he recalled his mother's thin frame and haggard look. He remembered the fear that would churn in him as he heard her coughing night after night.

In the midst of those years, there was really only one bright spot... the little church down the street. His mother started attending regularly with baby Carly and 10-year-old Sam in tow. The pastor and members there were kind and on more than one occasion helped the struggling family with groceries and household repairs. Sam enjoyed Sunday School and attended kids' events. He began to wonder if it was true what the Bible said, that God really did care about him and his family. Although if He did, Sam thought He could do a much better job of looking out for them. Nevertheless, at age 12, he prayed to ask Jesus to be his Savior. It seemed to be a necessary formality for church membership. But God had remained much like his human father, a reality, but not a Presence in his everyday life. His mom however, had gained a faith through those years that was strong and unshakeable. In spite of their tough situation, Sam

would hear her singing as she worked, and praying with Carly each night at bedtime. He had told her that he was too big to be tucked in and she didn't push it, but there were nights alone in his bed that he wished he had her praying by his side as well.

Then suddenly one spring day his mother announced that they had to move again. In Sam's mind that was the beginning of the end. They moved across town to an even smaller apartment and even poorer neighborhood and, just two months later, his mother was dead.

Sam, 18 by then and working any construction jobs he could find, managed to make the necessary funeral arrangements. He determined that he and his sister would make it on their own. Fall came and he enrolled Carly in school. He tried to portray maturity beyond his years and evidently it worked because school officials never questioned his age or why he was the sole supporter of an 8-year-old.

Seven years had passed since that sad time. Sam smiled as he realized that he and Carly had been on their own all these years. They had survived! That was quite an achievement. Carly, now 15, had the apartment's one bedroom to herself while he slept comfortably on the living room couch. She seemed to enjoy cooking meals and cleaning their tiny home. She sang the songs their mother had sung and insisted on praying at mealtimes. Every morning she prayed that Sam would feel Jesus' presence with him and that God would watch over and care for her brother. And without fail she told God she'd let Him take care of all of her problems that day. Sam was thankful for her positive attitude, as naïve as he judged it to be. He recognized with a gut-stabbing fear he'd grown accustomed to, that he and Carly had made it these many years, but they were always only one pay-check away from homelessness. Their survival was up to Sam... not God.

The bus slowed. It was his stop. Sam stood up. No more daydreaming. Sack on his shoulders, he strode down the city street to his new job. Only a month ago he had landed this position with Capital Builders, one of the city's largest construction firms. The company had been contracted to handle the renovation of a large downtown cathedral and its adjoining shelter. The job would take at least a year, maybe closer to two. As he passed the brightly-decorated shops, he thought that perhaps this Christmas, for the first time ever, he could afford to purchase something nice for Carly... something a teenage girl would like. Although it occurred to him he actually had no idea what a teenage girl would want.

As he approached the cathedral, he saw a group of early-bird volunteers busy erecting a life-size nativity scene on the small patch of lawn near the main entrance. It was a cold day and he felt rather sorry for

baby Jesus. The most scantily-clad of all the figures, the infant lay atop his bed of hay, arms open wide, exposed to the frigid elements.

"Hey Sam! Top of the mornin' to you! Hope you had your yeast and shoe polish! Want some coffee?" It was Jack, his red-haired Scottish boss. Sam had learned that Jack actually owned the construction firm and usually worked in a fancy office a few blocks away, trusting his foremen to supervise jobs on site. But Jack occasionally chose a project to personally oversee. This cathedral remodel was one such job… "to keep me in touch with the real world," as Jack put it. In just a month, Sam had come to really like the guy. And Jack seemed to pay particular attention to Sam, assigning him some of the more challenging jobs and personally training him in new skills. Although twice Sam's age, Jack connected with his men in a way that was direct and comfortable. Sam slid his sack from his shoulders, placing it on the ground behind the newly-erected manger. It was a protected area up against the building where all the guys piled their tool boxes and lunch bags.

Sam accepted the steaming cup. "And why should I have eaten yeast and shoe polish this morning?" Sam was getting used to Jack's one-liners by now.

"So you can *rise* and *shine*, of course!" Jack laughed. Sam rolled his eyes, grinned and gulped the

coffee. One by one the other crew members arrived and gathered around Jack to receive their job assignments for the day.

"I have one more happy note on which to start our day," Jack announced to his team before dismissing them to their tasks. "The kind folks who run the kitchen at the cathedral's shelter next door have issued an invitation. You are all welcome to eat your noon meal at the shelter from now until the job's completed... even Christmas Day if you don't have anywhere else to go. You don't have to do this of course, but it's free! And I know they always serve a good hot meal and... it's free! "

Sam was the first of the crew to pull his tools from his sack and get to work. For a moment he allowed himself to extend his earlier daydream... his life had been hard. It still was. But things were looking up a bit. He had a decent job with an extra-nice boss. He had a great kid sister. He would have better than a peanut butter sandwich for lunch. And Christmas was coming. For the first time in many years Sam dared to imagine a Christmas that might actually be a bit merry!

Jack was clanging a copper pipe, his signal to the crew for lunch break. Sam climbed nimbly down from the scaffolding, stashed his tools in his sack, slung it over his shoulder and entered the shelter's bright cafeteria. The smell of hot chili and cornbread was like a magnet and partially masked the smell of unwashed bodies. This free lunch was truly a great perk! Sam could care less that he would be dining with derelicts. After all, he and Carly had teetered on the edge of homelessness for many years. He felt an instant bond with these folks. Sam got in line, eager for some of that delicious-smelling chili.

"Hey look... dem two's twins!" Sam looked toward the voice. It belonged to a toothless guy already seated with his tray of food. He was pointing his spoon at Sam and then waving it toward some area behind the kitchen counter. Sam took a step out of line to look towards the kitchen. He caught a glimpse of a flannel shirt, the exact same plaid as his. It was on the turned back of one of the kitchen workers, obviously a female. How embar-rassing! Not only did he have a pink-sequined tool sack, now he was dressed like a girl. The men in the food line shuffled forward.

"No, no Senhor," another shelter resident boomed. "Deez two eez not twins... more like frijoles con arroz! No es verdad, Mac?" Laughter erupted throughout the room and Sam was flustered. What in the world were these

guys talking about? By now he had reached the head of the line.

Suddenly the flannel shirt turned and he understood. Silky skin the color of espresso with cream, a smile as dazzling as any dental poster's, eyes as merry as a Christmas elf's. She pushed up her matching flannel sleeve and extended a graceful hand to now beet-faced Sam.

"Hi! I'm Mac!" she introduced herself. "And you are...?"

"S-S-Sam." He finally managed to stammer. Then feeling it imperative to say something more, he blurted, "But you sure don't look like a Mac!" His face grew more beet-y.

The beautiful girl laughed comfortably. "Oh my real name's Mackenzie. My folks and closest friends call me Kenzie, but somehow here at the shelter I got labeled 'Mac' and it suits me fine."

"Do you live here... or around here?" Sam was now holding up the rest of the line and getting way too nosy, but he didn't want this conversation to end.

"No. I'm taking a year off college to volunteer here. Best decision I ever made!" Mac turned away to refill the bread basket.

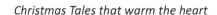

Sam seemed to have an extra burst of energy that afternoon, as his thoughts wandered frequently to his "twin" next door. For years he had been successful at keeping his mind off girls, other than Carly and his mother, of course. Their bare-bones lifestyle had long ago caused him to conclude that marriage would forever be a luxury he could not afford. But recently he had been noticing Carly's interest in *girl-stuff* and he felt completely inadequate to relate. He couldn't help but think it would be comforting to share life with a soft and gentle companion, one who could also be a female friend to his sister. Mac's exotic beauty had definitely wowed him. She was obviously a kind and pleasant sort... the kind of girl he really would like to get to know better.

"What am I thinking?" He scolded himself. "She's a college girl. I'm a common laborer. We are definitely not twins... not by any stretch of the imagination."

Nevertheless, Carly noticed something different when he arrived home that evening. "You've been smiling ever since you got home, Sam. Something good happen at work?"

"Actually, yes. I get to eat lunch at the shelter now. No more peanut butter sandwiches!" Sam was grateful for the convenient sidestep.

"Your smile's more than just a food-in-my-belly kind of smile." Carly looked intently at him. "Oh my! You

met a girl, didn't you!" It was more of an announcement than a question. "Hallelujah, the Lord is answering my prayer!" She jumped up and did a victory prance around the room.

"Wait just a minute there, Carly. I may have actually met a girl at lunch today... although how you knew that, I have no idea. But there's no way we would ever get together. So you need to quit your match-making right now!"

"*I'm* not match-making! *God* is and I've been praying for a long time that He would bring you a great wife. Maybe this is the one! What's her name?"

"Mac," Sam replied. "Do you really think God would match me with a girl named Mac?"

"You're right... not exactly what I had in mind," Carly said. "But I'm not going to stop praying! By the way, on a different subject... Sam, it's almost Christmas. Can we do anything special this year?"

"Now that you mention it, we have an invitation to eat Christmas dinner at the shelter and I was thinking that perhaps you'd like to attend the Christmas Eve service at the cathedral."

"Yes, yes, yes! That will be awesome! I think God's going to make this our best Christmas ever!" Carly gave another dance around the room.

Over the next three weeks, Sam started to think that perhaps he hadn't given enough credit to Carly and her prayers. Mac began joining him at his table when she finished dishing up food for the lunch line. Conversing with her was delightful, full of laughter and interesting stories of her time working in the city. She seemed to have an endless supply of *God stories*, as she called them... big and little ways she had seen God's apparent involvement in her work at the shelter. Her accounts of growing up in a loving family filled him with envy. Sam ventured to share with her just a little of his background and Mac seemed genuine in her sympathy, without being sappy. He found himself daydreaming on his bus rides to and from work each day about a future with Mackenzie. He realized he didn't even know her last name, but he knew that she was the kind of girl he could love for a lifetime.

A week before Christmas, as he finished his lunch with Mac, Sam summoned his courage. "Ummm Mac, would you be willing to help me pick out a gift for my sister, Carly? I'm at a bit of a loss to know what a teen-age girl would like."

"Sure, be glad to... when were you thinking of going?" Mac responded.

"Would tomorrow, after I get off work, suit?"

"Sure thing! I'll try to think up some possible gift ideas tonight."

"Perfect. See you tomorrow." Sam was ecstatic. He returned to work with even more gusto than usual. The afternoon hours flew by.

"Hey Sam. I need to talk to you a minute." Jack pulled the young man aside just before quitting time and handed him an envelope. It was pay day and Jack liked to personally hand his workers their pay-checks. "I've been meaning to have a little talk with you, Sam. Your workmanship just gets better and better. I like your willingness to learn and your habit of doing even more than is expected. I believe in rewarding good work. You'll notice a significant increase in this week's pay check. I want to keep you on my team for a very long time... if possible."

Sam's eyes widened. "I don't know what to say. Except... Thanks! Thanks so much Jack!"

"You're welcome. Just keep up the good work. And while you're at it, try to hang onto that goofy grin you've had on your face these last couple of weeks. It kind of cheers everybody up. Your smiley-ness wouldn't have anything to do with a girl would it?" He poked him play-fully in the ribs.

"Could be." Sam blushed. "She volunteers at the shelter. Her name is Mac. One of these days you should eat lunch there. Then you'd see why I'm smiling."

"Well…business at the company office usually keeps me occupied over lunch but I'd like to meet her," Jack replied. "Word is getting around and I hear she's pretty!"

"Pretty and pretty nice!" Sam replied. His expression changed. "But I'm afraid she's just too good for me."

"Listen to me, Sam. My wife Madge is wonderful and I *know* I don't deserve her! There isn't a man alive good enough to deserve a good woman. But guess what? There isn't a woman alive good enough for a good man either! I realized years ago that goodness isn't something any of us can claim. That's when I knew I needed Jesus in my life. I needed His forgiveness. I needed His help. I gave myself to Him and He's been helping me live my life ever since. Do you know what I'm talking about Sam?"

"Maybe. Sort of. Actually, I'm not sure. I prayed a prayer when I was a kid but I admit I haven't really felt all that close to Jesus. At least not the way you're talking about. And not the way my kid sister Carly seems to be. Besides, I've managed to survive decently well on my own. I figure Jesus is real, just not very real to me."

"Well, I'd love to see you do more than just survive." Jack put his hand on the young man's shoulder. "And there'd be no better time of year than Christmas to get reacquainted with God."

Sam couldn't wait to leave for work the next day. Having cashed his paycheck the evening before, he figured he would have enough money to buy Carly's gift after work and then, on his way home, he would stop by their landlord's house to pay this month's rent. And he might even have enough left to buy a small gift for Mac, and maybe even for Jack. The thought of being able to give to others filled him with joy. He put the money in his wallet and slid it into its protective pocket in the feed sack. Heaving the bag onto his back, he headed to the bus stop for his ride to the cathedral. He didn't even mind the pink sequins today. His world seemed brighter. More money, plus a date with Mac too! Sam could hardly wait for work to be over!

Quitting time finally came and Sam hurriedly packed his tools into his sack. He was about to sling it over his shoulder when he saw a shapely flannel shirt and wool cap coming towards him. She hadn't forgotten. He waved and strode towards Mac. Snow was beginning to fall and, as the two walked together, he felt like he was gliding on air. Her laughter, her gentleness, her enthusiasm for life... they were captivating. Snowflakes glistened on her black braids. She was beautiful inside and out!

In no time at all Mac pointed out a lovely silver bracelet in a shop window. She was certain Carly would like it. The price was right, but the shop had closed at five, so Sam decided he would stop by the next day over lunch to purchase it.

For a perfect end to a perfect day, Sam suggested they stop for hot chocolate. In the back booth of a quaint little diner, they sipped the cocoa and savored just being together. Once again Sam mustered his courage. "So Mac, I was thinking I would like to bring Carly to the Christmas Eve service at the cathedral and I was wondering if you would like to join us?"

"I'd love that! I volunteered to oversee the kitchen over the holidays, so I'll be staying at the shelter anyway. I can just meet you and Carly there." Mac's obvious eagerness caused Sam's heart to swell with hope. He wished he could stay and talk with her all evening, but he knew that wasn't an option and finally checked his watch. With great regret he realized he had to head home. He reached behind him to pull his wallet from its pocket inside his canvas bag when, with sickening dread, Sam realized there was no sack on his back. "Oh no! I must have left my sack at the job site," he exclaimed.

Humiliated, he asked Mac to pay for the hot chocolate, promising to repay her. They rushed out of

the diner and sprinted back to the cathedral, skidding to a stop behind the manger. Sam's face went as white as the falling snow when he saw what he had feared... the sack was gone! That sack was his survival. It was Carly's survival too. His tools, his rent payment, Carly's Christmas gift... everything had been in that precious bag! Just when things seemed to have been looking up, they plummeted to an ugly reality.

"I've got to get it back! I've *got* to get it back!" Sam paced back and forth in the powdery snow.

"I'm so sorry, Sam," Mac reached into her pocket and pulled out a ten-dollar bill. "This will get you home tonight and back to work tomorrow. I'll pray that somehow the Lord will help you through this. Have faith Sam," she said gently.

"You don't understand, Mac. My life has been one bad break after another. This probably doesn't seem like a huge loss to you, but that bag contains what I need to work, to live, to provide for my sister. How could I have been so careless to forget it? And why couldn't God have protected it for me? Every day it's been safe in that same spot while I worked. If God cares for me as much as you and Jack and Carly tell me He does, then why would He let some street thief carry my life away? I gotta go, Mac. I'll call the police when I get home and file a report. Maybe they can help. I've *got* to get it back! Good night Mac."

Sam sat, arms crossed, grim-faced, in the back corner of the bus. His mind was racing. Not with nostalgic memories of years past or with the recent lovely dreams for the future… but with the pain of an unjust present. Christmas surely wasn't looking very merry anymore.

The police report Sam filed amounted to nothing more than that… a report. "Did I really expect anything to come of it?" Sam thought cynically. Somehow he pushed himself through the next few days. But he was functioning under a fog of despair. Carly hadn't seemed the least bit concerned about the loss. He, on the other hand, could think of nothing else but the sack.

He and Carly had counted out the coins kept in a jar on their kitchen counter. They added up to just enough for bus fare to and from work for the next week, plus enough for bread, milk, eggs, and maybe some peanut butter.

"You see Sam, God will see us through. He always has and He'll do it again. Leave your old sack in His hands. He can bring it back if He wants, or make it up to you somehow." Carly's faith was unshakeable.

Mac had been just as optimistic. At lunch the day after the theft, she offered to float him a loan but Sam's pride prevented him from accepting her charity. Guys at work said he was welcome to borrow their tools until he could buy replacements and he had no choice but to accept their kindness. It was that or not be able to work. Even his landlord extended a one-month grace period.

Sam had to admit to himself that things could have been worse. But the theft of that sack was like a last straw. He was sick and tired of hardship, poverty and the constant worry about the "what-ifs" in his life. It seemed to him that the worst "what-ifs" anyone could imagine always happened to him. "Why did God let this happen? If He is so great, why hasn't He brought the sack back?

The days counted down to Christmas... Christmas, which had seemed so full of promise just a few days ago. Now it was a calendar day he wished he could skip.

Carly however, was not about to skip Christmas. "Sam, you promised that we could go to the Christmas Eve service at the cathedral this year and Christmas dinner at the shelter. We have enough money for the bus fare. I want to see all you've been doing at the cathedral. And of course I really, really want to meet Mac!"

"Listen Carly... Mac's just a friend. Only in fairy tales do guys like me marry smart girls like Mac and you know that fairy tales don't come true."

"You're right. Fairy tales *don't* come true. But maybe you and Mac aren't a fairy tale. Maybe you're a love story *God* is writing. Maybe... maybe not. But I at least want to meet her! You're *not* backing out on your promise, Sam!"

Consequently, Sam found himself seated between Carly and Mac in the hush of the grand cathedral waiting for the Christmas Eve service to begin.

"I'm sorry I roped you into attending this service, Mac," Sam whispered. "Probably, you'd rather have been with your family tonight."

"Oh no. They're attending a service at our home church, but we're all going to be together tomorrow. I really wanted to see what a service at a big city cathedral was like. And..." Mac paused and her eyes smiled their way into his heart. "... I wanted to spend Christmas Eve with you." She paused. "By the way, any news about your sack?

Sam's jaw tightened and he shook his head. "Nope." He was glad the pipe organ was beginning to play because he just didn't want to talk about the sack anymore. Mac would probably end up telling him to "give it

to God," just like Carly, and he wasn't up to a Christmas Eve lecture.

The choir rose to sing, O Come All Ye Faithful and Sam, feeling neither joyful nor triumphant, folded his arms across his chest and figured he could safely doze in the shadowy candlelight.

Later, Sam would conclude that he actually did sleep through most of that service but, sometime right near the end of the pastor's sermon, he was jolted awake by the most startling words, *"Folks... isn't it time you put all your cares and problems into* **one big sack** *and present that load of worries to Jesus? God gave His Son, so that we could have our burdens lifted. All He asks of us is that we give them all to Him."*

Sam faked a cough and whispered to Carly that he needed to get some water. He slipped out of the pew, buttoned his jacket and pushed open the heavy cathedral doors. Descending the church steps, his thoughts in turmoil, he plunked down on the bottom one. A light snow was falling and, if it wouldn't have been for his hard heart, it would have been an idyllic setting.

The pastor's words repeated themselves: "Isn't it time you put all your cares and problems into one big sack and present them to Jesus?" Sam put his elbows on his knees and rubbed his forehead with both hands. Jack's words came back, "There'd be no better time

of year to get reacquainted with God than Christmas, Sam."

As his cynicism and discouragement battled the truth he knew deep down, he became aware of the words of the choir's carol penetrating the night, "What can I give Him, poor as I am? If I were a shepherd, I would bring a lamb. If I were a wise man, I would do my part. Yet what can I give Him... give my heart."

"Okay God. I think I'm desperate. I prayed a long time ago, but I don't think I really meant it. Maybe I got You then, but You didn't get me. This time I really do mean it. I give You me... all of me. It's not much, but it's all I have to give. You gave Jesus. The least I can do is give You... me." Sam sat quietly in the starlight, savoring an unfamiliar peace and sense of God's presence. For the first time in his life, God felt real to Sam. A tear of happiness escaped from the corner of his eye.

Lifting his head, Sam surveyed the stable and the nativity figures surrounding the Infant in the feeding trough. A new awe of God and His amazing plan of redemption flooded Sam's heart. He wiped the tear from his face and, as he did, he caught a glimpse of something white, sticking out from under Jesus' wooden manger bed. He looked again. "Just a piece of trash the wind blew under there," he thought and walked over to remove it. As he stooped to grab the bit of white, he recognized immediately the corner of a canvas feed sack. Reaching excitedly under the manger, he pulled out his pink-sequined sack, now torn and empty. Or was it? Sam felt something hard as he ran his hands across the bag. He reached inside and, safe and sound in the denim pocket, obviously overlooked by the thief, was his wallet still filled with his December pay!

"Whoa God... this is unbelievable! You gave me my sack back!" Sam laughed out loud. "I gave me to You and You gave me my sack back! I don't believe it!"

The church bells began ringing out "Joy to the World." Sam ran his fingers over the pink sequins of his name and knew at that moment precisely where that sack belonged. Tenderly he bent over the Christ child and, as more tears flowed, Sam wrapped his beloved sack around the cold infant with the outstretched arms.

The cathedral doors swung open and his favorite two females were the first to emerge. Sam took two giant leaps towards them and, with a grin, wrapped an arm around both of them, lifting them off their feet and swinging them around. "Guess what? I don't need my sack back anymore. I don't need it *anymore!*"

"What? What are you talking about? What's happened to you?" Mac and Carly's questions were tumbling out.

"I said... I don't need my sack anymore!"

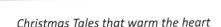

"Why not?" Mac persisted.

Sam turned and pointed at the manger. Like a spotlight, the moon shone on three sequined letters, S-A-M, now resting on the Christ child's chest. "Because I gave my sack... to *Him!*"

Christmas dinner at the shelter was amazing... turkey, mashed potatoes, cornbread filling, cookies galore. Sam and Carly worked alongside Mac dishing up the plates of food for the residents. Following the meal everyone, including the volunteers, got to pick a gift from under the tree. Sam laughed when he and Mac and Carly all unwrapped flannel shirts in the identical pattern.

"Triplets!" he announced with not a trace of embarrassment.

Games and carol singing followed and, as the residents began leaving, Sam and Mac and Carly headed to the kitchen to begin the clean-up.

Suddenly the side door flew open and a beaming lady entered, followed by Jack, lugging a huge shopping bag full of presents.

"Merry Christmas!" they shouted and immediately threw their arms around Mac in a giant group bear hug. Mac was laughing and hugging them back.

Sam stood holding a dishrag and looking completely confused.

Mac laughed more. "Sam, allow me to introduce my parents... my mother, Madge, and I think you already know my father!"

Madge held out her hand to Sam and Jack slapped him on the back. Sam still looked dumbfounded.

"But you don't look... I mean Mac, you're... well, you know... you don't look anything alike."

"Of course not. I was adopted. Twice actually. First by Jack and Madge and then by God. I have the best family in the whole universe!"

Sam felt a tap on his shoulder. "Oh, sorry Sis... This is Carly, my kid sister," Sam introduced the 15-year-old who was smiling a "this-is-better-than-a-fairy-tale" kind of smile.

"Hey... we'll help you clean up," Jack announced, "but first things first." He plunked the shopping bag on the kitchen counter. "Let's open the presents!"

Mac handed a small, silver-wrapped package to Sam. He read the tag, "To Carly, with love from Sam,"

and handed the gift to his sister. He shot a grateful grin to Mac. He knew before Carly tore the paper that it would contain the beautiful silver bracelet they had picked out together.

Sam glanced at Mac and mouthed, "Thank you. I owe you!"

"Glad to." Mac mouthed back.

A large heavy box was presented to Sam. It was marked, "From Jack and Madge." Sam unwrapped a for-real leather tool belt, complete with a set of every tool needed to replace his stolen ones, plus some new ones he could put to good use on the job.

Tears filled Sam's eyes and his voice choked. "You can't imagine what this means to me," he said. "I thought that I had lost everything when my sack was stolen. I even demanded that God give it back. But when I finally gave up and gave myself to Jesus, He gave me more back than I could have ever imagined possible. This has been an amazing and very, very merry Christmas!"

The happy group worked side by side washing dishes and restoring the shelter's cafeteria to order.

Sam and Mac tied up two large trash bags and headed out back to put them in the dumpster.

"Hey Mac... I want to see something." He grabbed her hand and pulled her around to the front of the cathedral. Sure enough, Sam's sack remained secure beneath the babe's outstretched arms.

"Just wanted to make sure Jesus still had my sack." Sam turned and looked tenderly at the lovely young woman by his side. "Like I said in the kitchen... this Christmas God gave me back more than I could have ever asked for. I consider your friendship one of His most special gifts. I like you a lot Mac. I hope that maybe our friendship can grow! Who knows where it might end up."

Mac removed her hand from his and walked to the manger.

"Oh no," Sam thought. "I've offended her! Did I come on too strong? I really don't know much about women," he lamented. But Sam said nothing and watched as the beautiful girl bent over the sack-clad baby. Picking up a hand-full of straw from the manger, Mac began carefully arranging the stalks, one by one, on the feed sack beneath the pink sequins. Sam approached quietly and peered over her shoulder. She was carefully placing sticks of straw on the sack, just below his name. Gradually he identified the letters she was forming and his face lit up as it dawned on him what this precious friend had spelled out!

She turned and slipped her hand into his. "Now we're together with Jesus, the best place in the world to be! I figure so long as we remain with Him, we can be sure He'll guide our future. Merry Christmas Sam! And if you don't mind... I mean, if you'd like to..." she paused, grinning and pointed to the word she had laid out in the manger. "I think you should start calling me K-E-N-Z-I-E... please call me Kenzie!"

All Santa Wanted

It had all started as a dare and, 50 years later, he was still at it. But now he was done. This year would be his last!

When one of Walter Nicholas' frat brothers teasingly nicknamed him "Saint" Nicholas all those decades ago, others chimed in and dared him to apply for the seasonal Santa job at the mall. Walt had no interest in children or in Christmas, for that matter. And he was about as far from being a saint as one could get, but he never backed down from a dare. So that's how it all began.

Being Santa became Walter Nicholas' yearly routine. He discovered quickly that the job came with some pretty nice perks. Initially it was easy extra income for a money-hungry college student. Walt could never get enough cash. A surprise benefit, he learned, was the great impression it made on the opposite gender. When he casually informed college girls that he spent his December playing Santa Claus for hundreds of children, they were immediately smitten. In fact, he credited that job with snagging his wife for him. He remembered Millie saying to him when he proposed, "I figure that anybody

who is willing to give joy to boys and girls at Christmas must be a good guy at heart." Millie was wrong. Little did she know that Walt had almost zero interest in the children who climbed onto his lap. The young Walter was an opportunist and being Santa was just a way for him to get what he wanted.

After graduation, he and Millie married and he plunged into a high-powered financial investment career. He no longer needed the extra money the part-time job paid. He intended to quit being Santa. But somehow the company president got wind of his after-hours job and expressed great admiration for such a worthy contribution to the community. Walt wanted to keep on the good side of his boss, so his Santa gig turned into a leg-up on the corporate ladder. Instead of impressing giggly sorority girls, he began to look for opportunities to casually let it slip to prospective clients what he did as a moonlighting job. Without fail, the information brought praise and affirmation and won him more than one lucrative account. Plus, the job provided him a never-ending supply of Christmas riddles and funny kid anecdotes that charmed more than one potential investor.

So what started out as just a joke, became a life-long habit. Not that Walt enjoyed it, because he didn't. He was kicked, poked, bit, and drooled on by multitudes of kids. He was even peed on. He detested the tantrums and the whining and the whisker-yanking. He forced fake smiles for photos. Luckily, the beard camouflaged his cynical sneer pretty well. But if playing Santa Claus served as a tool to gain greater respect from his customers and consequently greater success, Walt concluded it was worth enduring. So every year he repeated his Santa act.

Walt was a workaholic and perfectly content to fill his days with business pursuits. He had little time for Millie and was not thrilled when, ten years into their marriage, a daughter, Karyn arrived unexpectedly. He admitted that she was much cuter and smarter than the kids who gave him their lists each December but he was just too busy to pay much attention to her. As years passed, Millie and Karyn begged him to spend time with them but Walt was consumed with chasing down new clients or cooking up new ventures to bring in more money. Convinced he was being a good husband and father by providing a very comfortable life for his family, he packed every month with work. December was the worst of them all because, on top of his regular job, he held down the Santa job too. Millie and Karyn came to resent Christmas!

Millie was a faithful wife and loved Walt, sticking with him in spite of his self-centeredness. She continued to believe that somewhere hidden under his uncaring mask, was a soft heart. She was a strong Christian and talked to Walt about Jesus and His love. But Walt was

a self-made man and didn't see any need for a relationship with an invisible Deity.

Then, after 35 years together, Millie died. With her
mother's passing, Karyn moved away and quit commu-
nicating with her father altogether. Walt poured himself
even more into his work and tried to keep himself preoc-
cupied with any thoughts other than the years he had
wasted. But it seemed that every year his sorrow and
regret increased. Ten years passed. He was president of
his own corporation, richer than he had ever hoped to
be, but very much alone. Where had the years gone?

When he turned 70 the week before Thanksgiving,
the firm threw him a fancy retirement party, presented
him with an engraved plaque, showered him with a lot
of polite accolades, gave him an expensive watch and
said goodbye. He had no family and now he had no job,
except for being Santa. He loathed it more than he ever
had.

"I may as well get on with it," Walter muttered to
himself. "Thankfully this will be my last Black Friday as
Santa Claus!" He pulled the red cap onto his head. With
a scowl he put his arms through the sleeves of the heavy
red jacket and buttoned it. He picked a piece of lint from
the white fur trim on the cuff. He jammed his feet into
shiny black boots and took one final look in the mirror.
The fake beard and wig were no longer needed because

Walt's own wavy snow-white hair and bushy beard were perfect for the part and much more authentic-looking.

There was no Santa-like twinkle in his eyes but then, there never had been. He shook his head in disgust. He would do his duty and finish out this year but, with no motivation to impress others, he saw no reason to keep on being Santa in the future.

Walt left the house, squeezed his pillow-stuffed belly behind the wheel of his Lexus and headed for the first day of his last Christmas ordeal.

Walter Nicholas gave a perfunctory nod to the two young women who would be directing the children to Santa. The girls were dressed as toy soldiers, complete with red curly wigs poking out from beneath high furry black hats, their faces painted red white and blue, with enormous Pinocchio-like noses covering their own. Walt had to give credit to the mall for the great job they did each year with the costumes and North Pole scenery. He took his place on his golden Santa throne and braced himself for the Black Friday rush. "Let's get this show on the road," he barked with a reluctant thumbs up to his soldier helpers.

The lines seemed to get longer every year. And the children got ornery-er! When the first baby brought to him spewed half-digested breast milk all over him, Walt moaned inwardly. This was going to be a tough year. He knew it. As the morning progressed, he got requests for the most bizarre things... "a dollar-bill-dropping drone," "a robot doll that could repeat the alphabet in five languages," and "an automatic dog treat launcher toy." Gone were the requests for baby dolls, teddy bears, baseball gloves and Tinker Toys. It seemed to Walt that almost every Christmas wish was for something computerized, grotesque or violent. If he were honest, he would have to admit that there were still some decent, polite children who asked for innocent-enough things like rolls of Scotch tape, or tubs of Cool Whip. But they tended to get obliterated by the obnoxious little tyrants. Some of the children even brought along their lists, not written on paper in child-like scrawls, but displayed on the screen of their own smart phones. For *Saint* Nicholas, Walt thought some very sinner-like thoughts.

By late afternoon, Walt was in a sour mood. He looked at the line of waiting parents and children and frowned. Then he motioned impatiently for the next child in line.

It was a boy, cappuccino-skinned, with black wavy hair and chestnut-colored eyes. He looked foreign to Walt... maybe Middle-Eastern... maybe Italian... maybe

Spanish. Walt wasn't very good at geography. The youngster approached Walt with a confident stride and stood directly in front of him.

"So what do you want?" Walt had already dropped the jolly, "Ho-Ho-Ho... what can Santa bring you this Christmas?" He was a less-than-merry Santa for sure. But the boy seemed unintimidated.

"I don't want anything," the boy stated simply with a twinge of an accent.

"Well, you stood in line for an hour to talk to Santa... you must want something." Walt judged the boy to be about eight years old... the age many kids outgrew belief in Santa. He had talked to his share of smart-alecks who just wanted to make a mockery of Santa Claus. Walter figured he was about to be the butt of some disrespectful joke.

"No, I don't want anything," the boy repeated calmly and stared at Walt again.

"Do you think you've been bad and Santa won't bring anything for you?" Walt was getting frustrated.

"Oh no." The stare was penetrating.

"So why are you here?" Walt barked. "There are other children waiting."

"I came to ask you, Sir Santa, what *you* would like for Christmas." Walter blinked and tilted his head in confusion... it had been years since any child had addressed him as "Sir" and he couldn't remember a single child ever asking him what *he* wanted for Christmas. Walt was a little taken-off-guard. This boy was different. But time was passing quickly and the line was getting longer by the minute.

"I don't want anything," Walt retorted, "and if that's all you wanted to say, just turn and smile at the camera, and Miss Military over there will show you the way out.

"Okay." The boy gave a big grin, reached out to shake Walt's hand and then as an after-thought said, "Santa Sir, do you know how sheep in Mexico say, 'Merry Christmas'?" Without waiting for Walt to answer he said, "Fleece Navidad!" He threw back his head, laughed and left.

Walt watched him join a man who, he guessed, was his father. "Strange boy," Walt thought to himself as the two disappeared down a busy aisle. He turned his attention to the next cranky toddler but, for the rest of the day, he couldn't get that boy and his haunting question out of his mind.

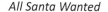

All Santa Wanted

December 3rd. A week had passed, along with several hundred gift-wanting children. Walter prepared himself for a second hectic holiday weekend and gave a reluctant signal to the toy soldiers to let the first child approach. In his mind, he was crossing off each day. He couldn't wait until he could hang up the red coat for good. The trouble was, he wasn't sure what he would do next. He had no family, no job, and no close friends. He missed Millie. She was always there when he got home. She was always singing Christmas carols and smiling. He hadn't realized just how much her peaceful presence meant to him, until it wasn't there anymore.

Walter shook himself back to the present and turned to face the first "brat" as he often mentally labelled the children lined up by the rail. By lunchtime he had been told that he really should go on a diet. Another sassy kid warned him that his use of reindeer for his sleigh was animal cruelty and he should be arrested. A bossy 10-year-old ordered him to not forget to bring batteries along this year. And yet another asked Walt to bring him a pair of pliers so he could pull out all his teeth, so the tooth fairy would bring him a lot of money.

By late afternoon, Walt was weary and longing for quitting time. For a brief moment, he propped his elbow on the arm of the throne and rubbed bushy eyebrows. When he looked up, he was looking straight into a chestnut gaze.

"It's you again," Walt stated. "So, ho-ho-ho… did you finally think what you would like Santa to bring you this year?"

"Oh, I don't want anything," the boy replied. "I came back to ask you, Santa Sir, what you would like for Christmas."

This kid was irritating. "Nothing! N-O-T-H-I-N-G… I want nothing! I am the one who brings the presents each Christmas… you know… the sleigh, the reindeer, the sliding down the chimney. It's my job and I'm good at it and… what's your name anyway?"

"Ori."

"Okay Ori… I don't know what you really want, coming here like this. *You're* not Santa Claus. I am! So smile for the camera and get going!"

Ori flashed a smile at the camera, but turned back to Walt. "Santa Sir, do you know where snowmen keep their money? In a snowbank!" He slapped his leg and laughed heartily, then grabbed Walt's gloved hand with both of his, shook it solidly, and rejoined his waiting father.

Walter motioned for the next child but his focus lingered on Ori as his black head faded from view. "I don't get him," Walter muttered under his breath. "Strange kid!" But as he greeted the next child, he realized he was feeling a little less mad, yet unexplainably, a little more sad.

Friday, December 10, arrived. For Walt, this was the halfway mark of the Christmas season. He was happy to be on the home stretch. Over the last couple of weeks, he had added more strange requests to his collection. One child had handed him a paper with ten long web addresses, so Santa could just order those items online and have them shipped directly to the child's address. Another told him to text her dad because he could forward Santa her entire list. And another boy, trying to be helpful to Santa, gave Walt the specific model number of a Droid phone and informed him it was available at the Verizon store at the mall.

"Oh my! Santa has sure hit the age of technology!" Walt lamented. It made him extra eager to be done with the whole business.

Just before his supper break, Walt saw the boy approaching. Outwardly he rolled his eyes, but he had secretly hoped the boy would come.

"Master Ori... you're back *again!*" Walter greeted him gruffly. "By the way... I'm curious... what's your nationality? I mean, were you born in the United States?"

"Oh no Santa Sir. I was born in Italy. But I live here now. And what is your nationality?"

"I'm Santa Clause. I don't have a nationality," Walt retorted impatiently.

"Oh, but you do," Ori announced. "You're North POLISH!" Ori giggled loudly. Walt was too used to being a grouchy Santa to join in Ori's laughter.

"Very funny," he growled. "I hope you've finally decided what you want me to bring you for Christmas."

Ori just stared at the old man for a moment. "I don't want anything, Sir Santa. I have so much already. What do *you* want for Christmas?" The boy's tone was almost pleading.

"Ori... you're a nice enough kid, but this is getting old..." Walt paused and then was surprised to hear himself mumble, "You can't give me what I want anyway!" His thoughts had suddenly turned to Millie and how much he missed her.... and his daughter and how he had driven her away with his neglect. But then he could have kicked himself. Why had he blurted out such a sentimental thing to this meddlesome young whipper snapper? "Look, I don't know why you keep coming back. I think you just need to tell your father over there to stop wasting his time and mine."

Familiar with the routine, the boy smiled for the camera. Then he reached for Walt's hand and squeezed it tightly. "Good-bye Santa Sir! I hope some day you will tell me what you want for Christmas! I will pray and ask Jesus to help you."

Then he skipped down the exit ramp.

"Oh great... a religious kid!" Walter muttered. He frowned as Ori and his dad disappeared into the crowds. But suddenly he remembered Millie and her prayers and he didn't want to admit it but, deep down, he knew he longed for both.

All week the boy kept coming to Walter's mind. His persistent question dominated Walt's thoughts... "What *did* he want?" He had spent almost an entire lifetime resenting the foolish wishes of others. But at the same time, he had feverishly pursued what he wanted, only to end up now feeling very empty. "What *did* he want?"

When the next Friday, December 17, arrived, Walt thought he was ready for Ori. As children filed through

his North Pole castle, he kept glancing over their shoulders, waiting for the khaki-skinned boy. He wasn't going to let this kid get to him. He would keep the upper hand. He mentally prepared the grilling he would give the child.

But Ori didn't come and, when it was time for Walter to take a Santa supper break, he delayed as long as possible, hoping the child would appear. He hurried through his meal and back to his post, for the first time in his long Christmas career, anxious to return to work. Still no Ori. Walt was bitterly disappointed.

Five minutes before mall closing, a panting, stocking-capped Ori came running towards Walt. Snow-flakes clung to his long eyelashes. His father, huffing and puffing, stopped at the gate of the castle to await his son.

"Oh Santa Sir," Ori stopped to catch his breath, "I was almost too late. I had a program practice at church. But now I am here!" The chestnut eyes bored into Walt's.

"Yes, I can see you are, Ori, and before you tell me again, I already know you don't want anything for Christmas, so I won't ask you. But today I have some other questions for you... "Do you know what fear of Santa Claus is called?" Walt tried to sound intimidating.

Ori looked puzzled for a moment then his mouth curled in a grin. "Yes, Santa Sir... that would be *Claus*trophobia!"

Walter was impressed. "How about this one... What do you call Santa if he goes down a lit chimney?"

Ori didn't miss a beat. "Krisp Kringle!" This time he chuckled.

Walt was enjoying pulling from his accumulated collection of Santa jokes and he figured, if he could keep firing riddles, Ori might be side-tracked from his usual question. "So, what do reindeer have that no other animals have?"

"Oh, Santa Sir... that is easy... Baby reindeer!"

"How do you know all these?" Walt asked.

"I google Santa jokes on the internet." Walter should have figured... technology. Then, before he could launch another riddle, Ori interjected. "I cannot stay any longer. My father said it is late and I need to get home. But please, Santa Sir... Jesus told me I should ask you again... What *do* you want for Christmas? Everybody tells Santa what *they* want. I wish someone would give Santa what *he* wants for a change."

"Sorry Buddy," Walter replied. "I don't have an answer for you." Then, seeing Ori's face fall, he continued with sudden tenderness... "but thanks for asking. Run

along now!" Walt reached out his hand to Ori who shook it respectfully, posed briefly for the camera and hurried off to his waiting father.

Walter Nicholas put up the "Santa will be back at 10 AM sign," said goodnight to the toy soldiers who waved merrily at him, and trudged to the parking lot. He had lied to the boy. He did have an answer to that question, but he didn't want to admit it to himself, let alone to a peculiar kid.

Friday, December 24. Walter was sad. He had thought he would be ecstatic about his last day as Santa Claus, but he was actually feeling downright depressed. At least this job gave him something to do. After today, he would have no purpose. And in spite of the thousands of children he had interacted with, he realized that he had been a big fake all along. He hadn't really cared about them but, now that he was about to lose them all forever, he suddenly wanted to hang onto them. All day Walter clung to each child a little longer than normal, feeling that as each one passed from his presence, he was losing more of himself.

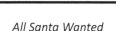

Being Christmas Eve, his shift would end at 5 o'clock… so Santa would have time to get to the North Pole to load his sleigh… at least that's the explanation the mall management put on the sign at the castle entrance.

Walt wanted to see Ori, but was doubtful the boy would come. He would probably be enjoying Christmas Eve festivities with his family. And Walt certainly couldn't blame him for giving up on such an uncooperative Scrooge of a Santa.

But at the stroke of five, Walt almost jumped off his throne! The final child of his career was walking towards him… a smiling little guy with wavy black hair and chestnut eyes.

"Ori! I am SO glad to see you! Ho! Ho! Ho! Can I bring you something for Christmas? I'll be loading my sleigh in a few hours you know."

"Oh Santa Sir… I don't want anything. Except…" Walter leaned in. "Except… I want to know what *you* want!"

Walter lowered his eyes. He couldn't face the soul-piercing gaze but he had to be honest with this child. "What I want, no one can give me Ori. What do I want? I want my wife Millie back! I want my life to count for something more than a big fat paycheck, a nice house

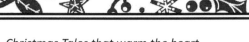

and car. I want to know what it is to love and be loved!" A tear ran down Santa's rouged cheek into his silver beard.

Ori stepped closer and held out a crookedly-folded paper. "Please, Sir Santa... my parents said I could invite you to our house tonight. This is the address. We will eat at 6:30. My mother makes delicious food from Italy. Later we will go to church. I will sing in the choir. Please come, Sir Santa... please!"

Ori threw his arms around Walt and gave the old man a big hug. He tucked the invitation paper into the patch pocket on the side of Walt's red coat. And with that the boy waved to the cameraman and ran off.

The toy soldiers put up the "Santa's gone to the North Pole... See you next year!" sign. Walter said a muffled "Merry Christmas" to the helpers and watched them hurry off into the crowds, no doubt on their way to family events. But Walter just stayed sitting, head down, wiping stray tears from his eyes.

Walt didn't want to go home. What was there to go home to? Reluctantly, he removed his Santa cap and stuffed it into his pocket. As he did, he felt Ori's invitation.

Walter pulled it out and unfolded it. It was obviously printed by the boy himself. Walter read, "Please

Sir Santa... I do want something for Christmas. I want to see you again. Please come to our house tonight at 6:30 PM. I do not want you to be late! 444 Holly Lane." And it was signed, "Your friend, Ori." A P.S. followed... "What's green, covered in tinsel and goes 'ribbet, ribbet?' Give up? A mistle-TOAD!"

Walter Nicholas laughed out loud and suddenly he knew precisely what he wanted to do. "After years of making promises I've known I could never keep... I can finally make one child's wish come true!" But he would have to hurry.

Walt became a Santa on a mission. He headed to a sports store and bought a baseball and glove, stopped at the toy store for a model airplane kit, the bookstore for a book of jokes for kids, and then, realizing he should also pick up something for Ori's parents, he selected a plaid cashmere scarf for the dad. He considered getting Ori's mother a scarf as well but then, out of the corner of his eye, he spied the music box store. He rushed over. There in the window was a glistening snow globe containing an intricately-carved nativity scene, complete with shepherds, angels, Mary, Joseph and of course baby Jesus. He hurried into the store and asked to see it. The clerk said it was the only one left. Walter cradled the fragile piece and then cautiously wound the gold key on the base. "Joy to the world, the Lord is come, let earth receive her King." The melody and words were ingrained

in his brain from years of background carols played at the mall, and the many years of hearing his dear Millie sing.

Walt looked out the door of the shop and fixed his attention on his Santa throne, now empty at the end of the corridor. Millie once told him that he had never truly put Jesus on the throne of his life. She had been right. Walter had made himself king and he realized now it had been a very costly mistake.

"Lord, forgive me," he whispered, clutching the Holy Family in his hands. "Jesus, please give this sinner a second chance!"

Paying quickly for the treasure, he made one more stop at the gift-wrapping station and dropped an extra-big donation for them to wrap the presents in record time. Walter looked at his watch. He had completed all the shopping in one hour. He strode to the exit. He would make it to Ori's house by 6:30!

But as the automatic doors slid open, Walter groaned. He hadn't realized it had started to snow... the asphalt was already coated. Traffic would be crawling. He wouldn't make it on time! "Lord, I know I don't deserve a Christmas miracle... but maybe You could help me out?"

Determined to fly, if necessary, Walter strode towards his car. He passed the city bus shelter without a glance at the crowd huddled beneath its roof. And suddenly through the wintry night, he heard a familiar voice.

"Sir Santa! Sir Santa!"

Walter stopped so quickly, his boots almost skidded out from under him. He turned to see Ori running towards him, arms open wide. Walter dropped his shopping bags and wrapped his Santa arms around the boy in a joyous hug.

"Ori... I was just on my way to your house. I wanted to give you what you wanted, but I thought I would be too late."

"And we missed our bus, so I thought I would miss you too!"

"Well, we can go together in my car!" Walter was almost giddy with happiness. "Where is your father?"

Ori turned and pointed towards the stable-shaped shelter and two figures stepped from the shadows into the snow-speckled light of the street lamp. The first one, Walt recognized immediately as Ori's dad and took a step towards him, hand outstretched for a formal introduction but then stopped abruptly.

Because, stepping hesitantly from behind her husband was a young woman with a red, white and blue painted face. Now minus the plastic Pinocchio nose, red curly wig and black furry hat, she looked completely different. Brown wavy hair spilled over her snow-covered shoulders. A sweet smile, so much like one he remembered, was illuminated by the moonlight and tears glistened with snowflakes on her cheeks. Walt stared in disbelief.

"Karyn! Karyn... Is it really you?" He thought he must be dreaming.

"Yes, Daddy... it's me!" She ran to him and buried her head on his thickly-padded shoulder.

Ori was hopping up and down with excitement. He bent over, scooped up mitten-fulls of snow and tossed them jubilantly into the night air. "It's even better than we prayed for! Jesus gave us the best Christmas ever! But I'm really freezing... and I'm really hungry too!"

"So what are we doing standing out here in this blizzard?" Walt exclaimed. "There's my car and I believe we're all headed the same place. Then we have some catching up to do!"

Ori and his dad climbed into the back of Walter's sedan and Karyn slid into the front beside her father. As they drove slowly through the snow-covered streets, intermixed with laughter and tears, Karyn's story unfolded.

"Daddy, I'm sorry for tricking you... but I wasn't sure you would want to see me again, considering the way I left when Mom died. I always resented how busy you were with your work and I decided I didn't need you in my life. So I accepted an offer for a job in Italy. That's where I met Nico. We married and then Ori came along and just a few months ago, we moved back here. Ori kept begging me to tell him about his grandpa and I realized that I never really knew much about you. When I was growing up I had always wanted so badly for you to enter my world, but never considered that I could have chosen to enter yours. So I applied for the toy soldier job at the North Pole."

"And I told Mommy I always wondered why nobody asks Saint Nicholas what he wants and so we got the idea that I could ask you myself!"

Two hours later a very happy family, now stuffed with incredibly delicious ravioli and cannolis gathered in front of the Christmas tree. Walter, still in his red Santa jacket, drew his cap from his pocket and fit it triumphantly on his white head. He stood up and turned to face the trio of loved ones snuggled on the sofa.

"Karyn... can you ever forgive me for being so consumed with *me* that I failed to see the treasure I had in you? You are so like your mother. I believe her many prayers for me were answered tonight. Nico... thank you

for loving my daughter and grandson and for making room in your heart for a sour old Santa. And Ori..." Walter choked up... "I don't deserve such an amazing grandchild. Thanks for not giving up on me!"

Then Walter presented three beautifully-wrapped packages to Ori.

"But Santa Sir... I mean Grandpa!" Ori corrected himself. "I told you I don't want anything for Christmas!" But he tore off the paper and was clearly delighted with each gift... especially the joke book. Nico expressed great appreciation for the scarf and, winding it around his neck with a dramatic flourish, posed for a smile-filled picture with his newly-acquired father-in-law. Then Karyn gingerly loosened the tape on her package, folded back the foil paper and reached into the box. She lifted the exquisite globe and held it up to the light. The silvery snow shimmered in the glow of the tree lights. She carefully wound the key and the lovely carol began playing.

Karyn sighed. "Dad... I believe the Lord Jesus has truly come and given us a second chance... starting tonight!"

"You're right Karyn... I know He has!" Walter Nicholas playfully ruffled Ori's wavy hair and, with the merriest twinkle in his own chestnut-colored eyes, proclaimed with certainty... "And that's *exactly what Santa wanted!*"

Yumi,
The Flea

Three eager children pushed and shoved each other, trying to snuggle as close to their grandfather as possible. There was just enough space on the oversized recliner for all of them to squeeze next to him. The lights of the Christmas tree twinkled while carols played softly in the background. It was Christmas Eve in the Sherman household and that always included a story told by the patriarch of the family. The elderly gentleman waited patiently for his grandchildren to stop *rutching* and settle down for the annual tale.

Alex was the big brother... now 10 years old, and he felt he was really too grown up for a children's story. Still, it was tradition and no one could tell stories like his grandfather. He straddled the arm of the chair, one foot dangling. If the story seemed too juvenile, Alex figured he could make an easy escape. Caroline was eight and still child-like enough to love make-believe. She tucked her arm under the old man's and leaned her curly head against his shoulder. And little Jo-Jo, the baby of the family at age "twee," believed he had lap privileges and plunked himself there, leaning back against his grandpa's broad chest. Their dad and

mother cuddled together on the sofa opposite, tired from all the Christmas rush, and savoring the opportunity to relax.

Grandfather began. "Children, I have something very important to show you." With great difficulty, because three pairs of arms and legs twined around him, he reached into his pocket and pulled out a brown, wrinkled walnut.

"Y-U-M-I," Alex read the four letters roughly inscribed on the shell.

"Yummy!" Caroline exclaimed. She was very proud of her reading ability.

"Well, almost, Caroline. It's actually pronounced Yoomy," their grandfather smiled.

"What's Yumi?" Jo-Jo asked.

"Ah...Yumi's in the nut," Grandpa whispered dramatically.

The three leaned in. They held their breath as he slowly lifted the top half of the shell.

Alex spoke first. "I don't see anything!" He bent close and, as far as he could make out, there was nothing but a piece of absorbent cotton in the bottom.

Caroline agreed. "It's empty, Grandpa."

Only Jo-Jo spotted the tiny speck of black in the middle of the cotton. "Dat's dirt!" he announced. Jo-Jo loved dirt of any kind... although usually in more than infinitesimal amounts.

"That's not dirt, Jo-Jo. That's a flea." the old man corrected. "A very special flea!"

Three noses pushed forward for a closer look.

"Oh come on Grandpa, what's so special about a flea? And it's a dead one too!" Alex rolled his eyes. He was sure he was too mature for a *flea* story. Nevertheless he stayed parked on the arm of the chair.

"Well, if that's the way you feel, I'll just put my flea friend back in my pocket. We can skip the story, if you'd like." And their grandfather began to close the walnut.

"No, please tell us!" Caroline urged. And Jo-Jo begged, "*Pease* Grandpa!"

"Well, all right!" The old man cradled the tiny treasure, with its tinier contents, in the palm of his hand and began his tale...

Yumi was a rascal right from the day he hatched. As a young larva, he could crawl farther and faster than any of his 10 brothers or 9 sisters. He was the first to spin his silken cocoon and the first to emerge as a young adult flea. Yumi had big plans.

For generations, his family had lived quite comfortably in the soft fur of a massive sheep dog named Samson. There was plenty of room for the whole flea clan to live comfortably burrowed into his hide. They could easily get all the blood they wanted for dinner and, except for having to dodge Samson's powerful left-leg scratches, life was pretty cushy for them all. When Samson went bounding through the fields, herding the unruly sheep for his master, the fleas hung on tight, laughing hysterically through their wild canine roller-coaster ride. They thought life could not be better.

Except for Yumi, that is. He always thought life could be better. He wasn't content to bump along on a ground critter for his whole life. He wanted to soar! He wanted to see the world. Residing on Samson, the only things he would see would be fields and silly sheep.

So when his family members were asleep, Yumi did some very daring things. On more than one occasion, he sneaked all the way to the end of Samson's bushy tail and hopped over to a sleeping herdsman. He took great delight, biting those poor men in some most embarrass-

ing places. He dodged their desperate scratches nimbly and simply skipped to another prime location to harass the worker and get a good feast besides. Human blood was a real treat for a flea... kind of like ice cream is to humans... so Yumi savored his midnight excursions to the sleeping shepherds. He was always careful to make it back home to Samson before the dog awakened. He would rejoin his sleeping family, snuggled in the cozy fur, chuckling to himself over his hilarious escapades.

Yumi was especially close to his one little sister, Ava. His other siblings just laughed at Yumi's big dreams. But Ava always listened and tagged along behind him when he paced impatiently from Samson's shaggy head to tail. "One day I'm going to fly, baby Sis," Yumi announced.

"If you fly, I want to go with you," Ava begged.

"We'll see," was all that Yumi said. He couldn't imagine Ava keeping up with him. After all, he could leap two hundred times the length of his body. He heard his father say that only frog hoppers could do better than that. Yumi was sure his little sister couldn't possibly jump as far or as high as he could.

One day Yumi was practicing his long jumps while Samson snoozed peacefully. The rest of the flea family members were also asleep, stuffed from the big juicy meal they had just enjoyed together. But Yumi wasn't

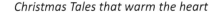

into after-dinner naps. He was a hyperactive flea who just couldn't sit still for long. All at once he realized that his chance for escape had come. A little sparrow had landed only inches from Samson's nose. If Yumi acted fast, he was sure he could jump right onto that bird and then... he'd be up, up, up and away! Without stopping to think a moment longer, he hopped to the end of the longest strand of fur on Samson's front paw. Then, springing with all his might, he launched himself towards the unsuspecting sparrow.

Yumi landed light as a feather on the sparrow's tail. "I did it!" he cried triumphantly. "Nothing will hold me back now." But suddenly he heard a little voice cry out...

"Catch me, Yumi! I'm coming with you!" And before he could open his mouth to protest, he saw Ava press herself down against Samson's foot and leap towards the sparrow. In a flash Yumi hopped to the tip of that sparrow's tail feather and reached as far as he could. With her little claw, Ava barely managed to snag one of the hairs on his extended leg and Yumi pulled her to safety. Then, before he could even scold her, the sparrow spread its wings and they were off! Yumi was flying... with his little sister clinging terrified to his leg.

For one flea-ting moment he considered shaking his leg. But no, he couldn't do that! Ava would fall to the ground and die! With herculean strength (for a flea, that is!), he drew his leg upwards and pulled his sister to safety.

Over the next several days, Yumi thought and thought and tried to figure out some way to get Ava back to their Samson address, but he couldn't come up with a solution. Having his baby sister tagging along would definitely cramp his style. He wanted adventure. He wanted to tour the globe...by himself! But it appeared he was stuck with Ava, so he would just have to make the best of things. They would travel the world together.

And so they did. Now, hitching a ride on a sparrow certainly wasn't flying first class... sparrow travel was pretty ordinary... kind of like flying economy. Still, for Yumi and Ava who had never been more than a few feet off the ground, sparrow travel was amazing. They saw hills and valleys, meadows and rivers. They swung in tree tops and perched on fence posts. They saw sights they had never seen before... towns and busy streets and all kinds of animals and people... not just silly sheep and dirty shepherds. Yumi found that it was actually kind of nice to be able to share his adventure with Ava. She wasn't really cramping his style too much. Yumi finally began to think that his life could not be better.

What he didn't know was that his life was about to get a whole lot worse!

After a particularly exciting day gliding around the countryside, the sparrow came to roost on a pillar in a

town's public square. Yumi and Ava had a good meal of sparrow blood and Ava settled down in the soft fuzz behind the sparrow's head (he couldn't twist his head around to peck at her there) for a nice nap. Yumi of course wasn't into napping. He began his daily *air-obic* exercise. He was quite proud of how he could leap straight up and come right back down on the same spot on the sparrow... a much smaller target than Samson had been. Yumi was a good *ath-fleat* and he prided himself in his strength and skill.

But suddenly, when he was right in the middle of one of his long jumps, the snoozing sparrow awoke with a start and, with a frantic flapping of wings, took to the air. In seconds, that sparrow, along with Ava, his unsuspecting, sleeping passenger, was soaring upwards. Yumi reached desperately towards the bird, extending his hairy leg to try to catch a tail feather. He clawed at the air, but that sparrow flew right out from under him. Yumi came crashing to the cobblestone below with a flea-sized thud. He looked up in horror to see the sparrow, with his darling little sister Ava, disappearing into the sunset. The future suddenly didn't seem nearly so exciting to Yumi!

Life changed for Yumi that day. He had landed on the dusty stones of a large courtyard. If he was to survive, he had to find something to eat... that meant finding an animal or a human being. But he had hurt his leg in the fall, and could only limp along. He trudged dejectedly across the town square. Now the big world didn't seem so thrilling. Now, being safe and sound at home on Samson with *all* his family was all he wanted. No matter how hard he tried, he just couldn't seem to grab onto a passing foot. He began to fear that he might die of starvation. He grew weaker by the hour. Just when he was about to give up in despair, a small burro and his owner stopped momentarily right beside Yumi. Frantically summoning the last of what little strength he had left, Yumi crawled exhausted onto the leg of that little donkey. He clung desperately to a clump of fur and managed to get his first life-saving sip of blood. As his strength returned, Yumi limped his way to the burro's head and finally stationed himself on the tip of the donkey's longest ear. From there, he would have the best view of the surrounding area.

For days he hoped that the sparrow would return with his precious Ava. But weeks passed and Yumi knew he would never see his sister or his other siblings again.

Yumi learned that the little burro's name was Toby and, since the lonely flea had his ear, Yumi began talking to Toby and pouring out his sad story. Toby listened sympathetically and didn't seem to mind one bit that he was hosting a flea. The two struck up a friendship. Many days, Toby's owner would lead him into town to buy supplies. The owner was a kind man who often talked aloud to his little donkey as he walked beside him. Yumi was sad to be without Ava but listening to Toby's master helped take his mind off his sorrow. Yumi had never been a religious flea. He had never actually thought much about how he had come to be hatched or what his purpose was in the world. But Toby's owner was obviously a very devout person and often thanked God for blessing him with such a fine pack-animal as Toby. Yumi began to wonder if anyone would ever feel like thanking God for him. After all, he was just a teeny, tiny flea and one that had taken great delight in being a pest. Even worse than that, he had been critical of his family, deserted them and failed them miserably!

One day as they walked to town, Yumi smelled a horrible smell and tried to squish further down into Toby's fur, so as to block out the foul odor.

"Whew! Our Greek neighbors must be spreading their pig manure on their fields today," the kind man said. "Pigs are definitely not kosher animals, Toby… you'll never find one at my house. They like to roll around in the mud. I've heard they do it to keep cool… but good motive or not, they're still covered in mud. And eating their meat isn't good for you… high fat content I think. Sometimes I wonder why God even made animals like pigs. Maybe someday He'll explain it to me, Toby. What do you think? Oh, that's right… donkeys can't talk… although I heard of one who did." And the man chuckled to himself.

"Actually Toby," he continued, "there will be a lot of things I'll want God to explain to me someday… like why was I born? Why would He choose me, just a simple woodworker for something great? Why me, my furry friend? Can you give me an answer? No, I didn't think so. Be glad you don't have to figure it all out, Toby."

The kind man patted the burro affectionately and rambled on and, although he had only a flea-sized brain, Yumi began to ask himself questions about his own life. "What did God want from him? Could God have any great plan for a flea with a bum leg and no family?" He wasn't sure, but one thing Yumi knew… he agreed completely that a pig was one animal he would stay far away from. "Pee-eew!" Yumi decided he would be a Jewish flea.

Yumi loved hearing the kind man talk about God… and even *to* God. He talked to God like He was a good Friend… although definitely invisible. Yumi started thinking that perhaps he could dare to talk to God too!

One morning, hours before sun-up, the kind man loaded Toby with all kinds of saddle bags and blankets. He led the little donkey (with Yumi riding just behind a pointy ear) out of their barnyard. Down a narrow cobble-stone street and then they were joined by a young girl. Loving hugs exchanged between her and her parents and they were soon leaving the older couple behind and heading out of town. Yumi couldn't help but think back to when he left his home. He hadn't even said good-bye. He was so concerned about finding his own excitement. Now he wished he could have even one hairy hug from his mother or father and especially from Ava.

Toby didn't soar like the sparrow and he didn't run and bound like Samson. Toby just kind of plodded along. Yumi had little choice but to plod along with him and with the kind man and the pretty young girl named Miryam.

It seemed they walked for days. Yumi had it easy, riding high on Toby's head. But the man and the lady trudged on, mile after mile. They had to be tired. The lady appeared to be reaching a point of exhaustion. Yumi knew that feeling. He scanned the horizon for any sign of civilization. Far in the distance, Yumi finally spotted a little village and he heard the kind man say, "There it is Miryam... the end of our journey." Then under his breath he added, "or maybe just the beginning."

Suddenly Toby's master stopped the little animal. He hurriedly rearranged some of the saddle bags and blankets (Yumi wiggled deeper in Toby's fur, to avoid being accidentally knocked from his perch) and then he gently lifted the young woman onto Toby's strong back. "At least the last part of the trip will be a little easier for her," Yumi thought.

But the last part of the journey seemed to be the hardest. The kind man kept Toby going so slowly. Yumi, who like males of every species, loved speedy modes of transportation, was tired of moving at a snail's pace. And when they finally entered the town, they stopped at house after house, knocking on one door after another. The kind man always turned away, looking so dejected and worried. "Didn't they have an address? Why were they here, anyway? What were they looking for?" It seemed like neither the kind man, nor the young lady knew exactly what they were doing.

As darkness descended, Yumi heard the kind man say, "It's better than sleeping out in the fields, Miryam. I know they're not Jewish, but everything will be okay. You'll see." And with that, they entered a little shack behind one of the village houses. The kind man laid a blanket over the straw in a long feeding trough and made a bed... if you could call it that... for his companion. Then he brought hay and water for Toby. Yumi yawned. "I have no idea where we are," he thought, "but

I'm too tired to care." Yumi took only a snack-size sip of donkey blood and fell fast asleep in Toby's soft fur.

When Yumi awoke a few hours later, he thought he must be dreaming. It was the middle of the night but the stable seemed abuzz with activity. Two torches illumined the run-down shelter. He could hear voices and movement and he limped as quickly as he could to the tip top of Toby's right ear. He looked around for the kind man and Miryam, but some burly shoulders blocked his view.

"Toby," Yumi whispered in the burro's ear. "You awake? Move over there between those guys so we can see what's going on."

The burrow yawned, but took a few wobbly steps toward the rough-clad men and then nosed his way between two of them. Yumi looked around. "Just a bunch of dirty old shepherds, probably trying to get out of the cold, just like us," the little flea concluded. He scanned the room for the kind man and Miryam. "Were these ruffians going to kick them out?" he wondered anxiously. But no, they seemed calm, and they all appeared to be focused on something. Yumi stood on tip toe and strained to see.

"Ah, that's better!" Finally he could see the kind man, with a tender smile on his face. Yumi remembered his father looking at his mother that way sometimes. He stretched a little more and then he spotted Miryam, still resting on her bed of straw but, beside her, curled in the protecting curve of her slender arm, lay a tiny bundle. It was... a baby!

"Where did that thing come from?" Yumi wondered. Then, "Mmmm, a baby. I remember my parents saying that baby's blood is very tasty. And I'd be ready for breakfast!"

Yumi was just about to ask Toby to lower him next to the baby so he could slide down for a sip when a low growl caught his attention. Something about that growl sounded vaguely familiar. He looked past the dirty man on his right and... "Could it be?" He blinked twice to make sure he was seeing clearly.

There in the stable was Samson! Samson! Yumi had been sure he would never see Samson again. He blinked and let his eyes move from Samson's furry face to his back. Was he dreaming? No! This was real! There lined up in single flea file were his mother and father and his brothers and sisters! Bad leg or not, Yumi knew what he had to do. "Please help me, God!" he prayed. Mustering all his flea strength, with one flying long jump Yumi landed smack on Samson's forehead and in a nano-second he was being bug-hugged by every wonderful member of the flea family! Except of course, for Ava.

"What happened to you?" "We thought we'd never see you again!" "You were gone so long!" "Where did you

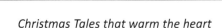

livc?" "Are you okay?" The questions from his family tumbled out... and then the one he dreaded. "Where's Ava?"

Yumi hung his head. No excitement or adventure in the world seemed attractive to him now. Reluctantly, he began to answer his loved ones... "Ava? Well you see, we lived on this sparrow and then one day..." tears began to drop from Yumi's eyes onto Samson. How could he tell his family that he had caused Ava's death? "And then one day..." He tried to continue, but his voice choked with a sob.

"And then one day, I fell into a Greek barnyard!" a sweet feminine flea voice cut through the air with a giggle. Yumi couldn't believe it! He and his father and mother and siblings turned, and there shoving its nose between the kind man and Miryam was a barrel-sized pig! And standing on the tip of its muddy snout was Ava!

One more heroic leap landed Yumi on that pig and then the brother and sister were laughing and hugging and crying all at the same time.

In a moment Yumi wiped away his tears and looked around. What a scene! How could this have all come about? Something in his flea-sized heart told him that God had made this all happen, and somehow He had used this tiny newborn baby to give a foolish little flea and his family a second chance.

Toby the burro looked fondly at Yumi. "You're sitting on a *pig*, Yumi! Hop on down to the baby and have a feast!"

"Nah," Yumi responded looking at the peaceful child sleeping by his mother. "I think that baby's blood is destined for greater things. And besides..." Yumi grinned at the dirty, muddy pig and then looked tenderly at his smiling baby sister, "Love beats kosher any day!"

"And they all lived happily ever after?" Caroline asked.

"Well, pretty much." her grandfather responded. "Yumi and his family ended up moving to a new home... on Toby! They had lots more amazing adventures together with baby Jesus and his family. Because you see, life with Jesus is the best adventure anyone could ever have!"

Caroline reached up and gave the white-haired old man a big hug. "Thank you Grandpa!"

"Me like dat stor-wy Gwanpa!" Jo-Jo bounced on his grandfather's lap.

"Yeah, that was a pretty good yarn Grandpa," Alex admitted... but you can't tell me that flea you're holding is Yumi.

"Oh no," the wise old gentleman replied. "This is Yumi the eight thousand, two hundred and fifty-sixth. It was his ancestor two millenniums ago that gazed at the baby Jesus in that flea-ridden manger. But keeping this walnut in my pocket helps me remember that if Jesus came to bring hope and a second chance to a *flea*... how much more He wants to do that for you and me."

"Yumi! Yumi!" Jo-Jo exclaimed. "Jesus an' You-me!" He pointed his chubby finger at his grandfather, then himself. Grandpa's eyes twinkled.

"Yes, Jo-Jo, there's a little bit of you and me in that flea. And Jesus will make all the difference in our lives, no matter how badly we've messed up, when we find Him and stick with Him."

He slid the walnut into his pocket and patted each child affectionately. "So that, my wonderful grandchildren..." he chuckled, and winked at the adults, "is the Christmas story... *in a nutshell!*"

Something Much Better

The *good old days*... a time many years ago when life was simpler. Cars were just becoming plentiful. Airplanes were newly-invented and literally just getting off the ground. And having a telephone was a real luxury. There were no TV'S, computers, DVD's, or cell phones. It was a safer era when a stranger wasn't someone to run from or fear but a person who could be smiled at and trusted. He was just a friend waiting to be met.

My father turned out to be that kind of stranger.

He was a young man at the time. It was December 23rd and he hopped into his brand new Model T Ford. He was going Christmas shopping! In those days, most people waited to do their shopping until just a day or two before the holiday. Stores stayed open very late Christmas Eve so many folks did all their gift-buying that night. There were no malls or outlet centers... only lovely old shops on the Main Street of the city. So people had to deal with wintery weather when they headed out to make their purchases. They bundled up... the whole bit... heavy coats, wool hats, scarves, gloves and sturdy snow boots.

My Dad must have looked like an over-stuffed teddy bear in all his winter wraps. He was comfortably warm as he chugged along in his beloved automobile. Most cars didn't have heaters but at least the roof protected passengers from falling snow or rain. He was feeling very eager to get his shopping finished so he could go home for the night, put his feet up and relax.

He parked the car along one of the busy streets. Crowded parking lots and multi-level garages didn't even exist. Snow was falling lightly on already-snow-covered sidewalks and shoppers were scurrying by, their arms loaded with packages. The Salvation Army lady under her big black bonnet was jingling her brass bell by the little box at the corner. Many folks paused, dropped in a couple of coins and hurried off again as she called after them, "Thank you very much! God bless you!"

Dad rushed along too. First to the china shop to buy a pretty hand-painted plate for his mother, then on to the department store to pick out a nice warm muffler (scarf) for his brother. Finally a stop at the market square to get fresh fruit baskets for his sisters' families. His father had died years ago, back in England. How he would have loved this new country and the wonderful family Christmas celebrations. Dad missed his father terribly but was glad the rest of the family could be together for the holiday. He pictured the decorated tree at home in the parlor. It was dazzlingly beautiful... new twinkling lights and delicate glass ornaments, and those silvery icicles which he had added himself. Oh, he could hardly wait to get home and sit awhile in front of that tree!

Toting the numerous bags filled with his precious purchases, he headed back towards his car. By this time snow was falling faster and the streets seemed much more crowded with people. He strode back across the market, bumping into shoppers. He saw the freshly-dressed turkeys hanging at the farmers' stands. Mmmm! He could almost taste his mother's delicious Christmas Day feast! He noticed a few Christmas trees still leaning against a fence. Most people had their tree by now but there were always those few procrastinators who would wait until the last minute.

He reached his car and loaded the packages safely in the back seat. Then he brushed the snow from the windshield and slid into the driver's seat. Brrr! It was really getting cold. A couple of groans of the starter and the engine roared to life. That was certainly something to be happy about on such a frigid, wintry night!

He pulled carefully out into the street... didn't want another automobile sliding into his precious Model T on these slippery, snow-covered roads. "Guess I should take it slow," he advised himself.

As he was inching along, he saw them... two of the poorest little urchins he'd ever seen! The boy couldn't have been more than eight and the girl looked about five. Their coats were ragged and stained. They had no hats at all! The girl's brown braids were sprinkled with snowflakes and looked like two frozen twigs hanging from her head. Her hands were stuffed into half-torn pockets. She probably had no mittens. She was slipping and sliding in smooth-soled, worn-out, over-sized shoes as she tried to keep up with her brother. He also had no boots or mittens but he couldn't stuff his hands in his pockets because they were tightly grasping the base of the sorriest-looking Christmas tree you ever did see! In fact, at first glance my father thought the boy was dragging a long tree trunk. But when he looked again he realized there were a few measly branches sticking out here and there with some stubborn needles still clinging to them.

"Where in the world did those children get a tree like that?" Dad muttered to himself. "Why, it would be better used for firewood than a Christmas tree! I can't imagine anyone wanting that thing in their living room." And then he got an idea!

Pulling over to the curb just ahead of where the children were struggling along, he jumped out and went around to the sidewalk to meet them as they trudged forward with their precious load.

He could see them more clearly now. The boy had freckles all over his face and his red-brown hair was thick and wavy. He was huffing and puffing. It was no easy task to lug even this spindly tree along in the snow. But he had a determined look. The little girl appeared half-frozen yet her jaw was set firmly too, intent on keeping up with her brother.

"Probably immigrant children," Dad concluded as he watched them approaching. Only nine years earlier he had been one of those children, struggling to help his family survive in a new country. His heart went out to them.

"Hey there children! Merry Christmas!" he greeted them as they reached the spot where he stood.

They looked up startled, stopping right in front of him. The boy shaded his eyes from the falling snowflakes and looked cheerfully at my Dad. "Merry Christmas to you too, Sir!" No mistaking, it was an Irish accent.

"Yeth, Merry Cwithmuth, Mithter!" his little sister added through chattering teeth.

"I see you have a... a Christmas tree there!" Dad hesitated a bit on the word *Christmas*... it hardly looked fit for a celebration.

"Yes, Sir!" the boy answered proudly. "We bought it ourselves!"

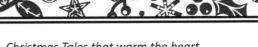

"If you don't mind my asking, where did young folks like yourselves get enough money to buy a Christmas tree?"

It was the little girl who piped up. "We earned it ourthelvth... shov'llin thnow and deliv'rin packageth for our neighbor!"

"It doesn't look like much, I know," the boy added, "but it was all we could afford and Mother and Daddy will be really surprised."

My father looked gently down at the children and smiled. "And who are your parents?"

"Patrick and Mary O'Shane... and I'm Patrick Junior and this is Celia." The young man patted his sister good-naturedly.

"Well, Patrick and Celia O'Shane, I'd like to make you an offer," Dad stated in a friendly but business-like way. "I have at my house right now a big bushy Scotch pine tree. It is leaning against the rail on my back porch. It just so happens that my boss gave it to me yesterday, thinking that I didn't have a Christmas tree. However, I already have a lovely one all decorated in our parlor. I've been wondering what to do with that extra tree."

Patrick's and Celia's eyes grew big as saucers as they guessed what he was about to say.

"But Sir, we spent all our money on *this* tree. We can't buy another one," Patrick replied respectfully.

"Oh, I'm not planning to sell my tree," Dad went on. "It was given to me, so I want to give it to someone who would enjoy it." He paused for a moment and eyed the children. Would they be willing to give up the tree they were grasping so tightly for a tree they had never seen and which was offered to them by a total stranger?

"Children, if you will throw away this tree and come with me, we'll get my tree and take it to your house. It's yours if you want it!"

Dad always told me later that he expected the children to hesitate and maybe even decline his offer, so he was amazed at their immediate response.

Without even the slightest hesitation Patrick blurted, "Where shall I throw this one, Sir?"

Dad smiled at the boy's eagerness. "Look, just over there by that building there's a pile of trash; just toss it there. Someone will be glad to use it for firewood."

Slipping and sliding, Patrick dragged the tree over to the pile. Then he turned around, took two running steps and slid the rest of the way back on the snow. He laughed as he reached my father and took Celia's hand. She looked up at my Dad and grinned through her shivers, showing two missing front teeth.

"Okay O'Shanes, let's go!" They all piled eagerly into the Model T and, in no time at all, were back at Dad's house loading the gorgeous tree onto the top of the car. Dad even threw in a box of Christmas cookies he had received at work plus the half-full box of silvery icicles the children could use to decorate the splendid pine. The children were speechless. Their faces shone with happiness and excitement.

Patrick stood on the wide running board so he could help hold the tree as the three of them wound back through the city streets to the O'Shane home.

My father helped the children carry their treasure up the long flight of steps to their tiny second-floor apartment.

"I'll leave you now children, so you can go in and surprise your parents," he whispered as they reached the shabby door of their flat. "Merry Christmas to you all!"

For the rest of his life he would always remember the expressions of joy and gratitude on Patrick's and Celia's faces as they whispered back, *"And a very Merry Christmas to you too, Sir! Thank you so much!"*

As he made his way home that cold night, his heart felt warm, the way it always does when a kindness is shown. And when he finally settled down on the old

rocker in the parlor, he gazed at his own brightly-decorated tree. His thoughts replayed the events of the evening. He shook his head when he considered just how much those dear children needed to trust him in order to throw away their prized tree in exchange for the yet-unseen one he offered to them.

Suddenly he knew that, in the events of that snowy night, God had planned a lesson *for him*. For years he had clung to his sinful ways. If he was objective, he had to admit to himself that his life was pretty empty and meaningless. He knew the Lord Jesus had come to him over and over and held out the offer of eternal life, forgiveness of sins, abundant joy and purpose. He could have it all, if he would just turn his back on his old ways and receive Jesus' free gift. But he had stubbornly refused. Time and time again he had refused. He saw himself now as so very poor and foolish!

"Where shall I throw it Lord?" he whispered. "I don't want this weight of sin anymore. I want *You!* Forgive me for holding onto that which is so worthless in light of eternity. I receive Your gift!"

A silent tear fell on his hand. He reached over and picked up the old leather Bible from the shelf. He wanted to read the Christmas story. Somehow he knew it would seem wonderfully different tonight.

"Patrick and Celia O'Shane," he muttered under his breath, "You thought I gave you an incredible gift this Christmas... but," and he grinned, "bless you both... you gave me something... *so much better!*"

Author's Note

My father told this story often as I was growing up and I love to tell it now to my own children and grand-children. Like the two trusting children, my dad threw away the old to receive something so much better. His life was never the same.

In the hustle and bustle of our hectic lives, how good it is to slow down and reflect on the greatness of God's free gift to us. How pitiful is the *stuff* we treasure, compared to the riches He is waiting to give us. How foolish to carry the weight of worry and fear when He is ready to give us hope and joy and peace instead. How sad to struggle under the guilt of sin, when He holds out to us the glorious freedom of forgiveness!

As we open our gifts Christmas morning and smile with delight over toys and electronic games and new clothes and all sorts of fancy presents, may we all pause to remember that all these things are little better than an old spindly Christmas tree. Jesus has **something so much better** to offer us all!

For God so loved the world
that he gave his one and only Son,
that whoever believes in him
shall not perish
but have eternal life.

John 3:16

Made in the USA
Lexington, KY
03 December 2019